ROSIE

and

SKATE

ROSIE (and) SKATE

BETH ANN BAUMAN

WENDY
LAMB
BOOKS

Visit us on the Web! www.randomhouse.com/teens

Educators and librarians, for a variety of teaching tools, visit us at www.randomhouse.com/teachers

Library of Congress Cataloging-in-Publication Data
Bauman, Beth Ann.
Rosie & Skate / Beth Ann Bauman. — 1st ed.
p. cm.
Summary: New Jersey sisters Rosie, aged fifteen, and Skate, aged sixteen, cope differently with their father's alcoholism and incarceration, but manage to stay close to one another as they strive to lead normal lives and find hope for the future.
ISBN 978-0-385-73735-7 (hc) — ISBN 978-0-385-90660-9 (lib. bdg.) — ISBN 978-0-375-89390-2 (e-book) [1. Alcoholism—Fiction. 2. Sisters—Fiction. 3. Fathers and daughters—Fiction. 4. Dating (Social customs)—Fiction. 5. Family life—New Jersey—Fiction. 6. Self-help groups—Fiction. 7. New Jersey—Fiction.] I. Title. II. Title: Rosie and Skate.
PZ7.B32743Ros 2009
[Fic]—dc22
2009010575
The text of this book is set in 13-point Bembo.
Book design by Kate Gartner
Printed in the United States of America
10 9 8 7 6 5 4 3 2 1
First Edition

With much love, for my mom, Irene Bauman,
who lost her mom when she was young

Rosie

My dad's a nice drunk. There is such a thing. I know how that sounds, but honestly he's a good person. My sister, Skate, is going to give you a different story, but I want you to hear my side too.

Before our dad went to jail three weeks ago, one of his favorite places was the old faded couch on the sunporch, where he'd lie with sandy feet, clutching his bottle of Old Crow whiskey, gurgling to himself with a dreamy smile. If he saw me standing above him, staring down at him, he'd give me a little finger wave. "Lovely to see ya, Rosie girl." Or sometimes he'd look at me and not see me at all, but he'd smile all the same. You see what I mean? Screwed-up, but nice.

Of course this isn't true of every drunk. This is what I've learned from coming to these meetings for the past three weeks: some drunks have a mean streak. The guy sitting across from me once had his nose broken when his dad blew a fuse. And some drunks are crybabies, I learned from a girl with a nose ring whose mom schleps around the house in a dirty bathrobe, moaning about the past. And some are hopeless, like the dad who gets out of rehab and then starts drinking the very next day. My dad—nice drunk that he is—is also hopeless, Skate says. Last time he went to rehab for six weeks and started drinking again the very same afternoon he came home. And some are sneaky; they go to work, pay the mortgage and gas bills, make spaghetti and meatballs, but they live in a boozy fog, hiding their bottles in the toilet tank, the hamper, the fireplace.

Skate hates these meetings. Drama Queen, she calls them. *"Please,"* she says. "All that yakking. All that whining." That's why she isn't here yet. I'm worried she won't come. I just come. I show up here in the basement of St. Joseph By the Sea and sit on a folding chair and eat Gus's cookies out of a shoe box lined with foil. Skechers, size 12. Gus is in college and runs the meetings. He makes butter cookies in the shapes of moons and stars. His mom gave him the cookie cutters, he told me. The cookies are dented and crumbly but sweet, and we all wind up wearing crumbs down the front of our shirts. So I come here every week and eat cookies and wear crumbs and listen to other kids whose parents are drunks.

Gus drags a chair over to the circle and starts the meeting. But I can barely pay attention to what he's saying. I sip a cup of cherry cola and stare at the door, willing it to swing open and blow in my sister—with her long wild hair and her skateboard under her arm. She's always late, if she comes at all. She thinks our dad is a big loser.

"My dad guzzles vodka down the bay," Nick says. "Drinks it in a teacup. Like he's some regular guy." Nick is a quiet kid from my homeroom, tall and slouchy with hair falling into his face. "The old dude sits there sipping vodka, getting up and down to refill his cup from the bottle he keeps hidden in cattails. Drinks till he passes out. Tips right over into the sand. Happens between nine and nine-thirty every night, like clockwork." Nick looks out at the room with a little frown and hooks his stringy hair behind his ears. He has the daintiest pink ears I've ever seen on a person. "So we head down there. My brothers grab his arms and my sister and I each grab a leg and we hoist him into a wheelbarrow and wheel him home."

"Why do you do that?" Gus asks.

"*Why?*" Nick says.

"Why?" Gus says calmly. Nothing ever rattles Gus. He has a nice sad smile, like he expects stuff to be totally screwed-up, even though he wishes it weren't. Gus is built like a wrestler—short but muscle-y, and he's got this spiky crew cut he runs his hand over when he's thinking hard.

"But we can't leave him there!" Nick blurts out, his little ears turning pinker.

"Why not?" Gus says.

And while I'm listening and not staring at the door, it opens. And here is Skate, carrying her board. She flashes a smile at the room and drops into the seat next to me. "Hey, Ro," she whispers, reaching for a cookie. She's wearing torn Levi's, fishnets, Keds, and a washed-out black T-shirt decorated with a tiny strawberry. Her long hair is beaded with drops of water.

"Where were you?" I whisper back, reaching for a cookie too.

"Let me get this straight," Nick says. "You think we should leave him there? Lying in the sand? Stupid drunk? For all the neighbors to see?"

"Yes," Gus says.

Nick stares at him. "Are you crazy?"

Gus smiles. "Occasionally. But really, why not leave him there?"

"Well, it's embarrassing!" A few of us nod in agreement.

"But it's your dad's problem, not yours," Gus says.

"But he's my *dad,* and I don't want the whole frickin' neighborhood to see him passed out on the sand."

"They probably see you loading him into the wheelbarrow."

"Maybe not," Nick mumbles. "Maybe not."

"If it happens almost every night, they probably know," Gus says.

Poor Nick. If I were him I'd probably hoist my dad

into a wheelbarrow too. I smile at him, but he's staring at the floor, his stringy hair falling into his face.

Our dad didn't pass out in the yard or at the beach or anything like that, but even so, drinking wrecked him. He went to Walgreens in his raincoat and slippers and shuffled down the aisles, loading the lining of his coat with crazy stuff: a can opener, coconut tanning oil, nail clippers, panty hose, potpourri. Then he stood in line, and when the cashier cracked a roll of quarters against the side of the register, he reached in and grabbed a stack of twenties. "Thank you, my dear," he said. There was no security guard working that day, and when the police caught up to him, he was sitting on the curb a block away, having just trimmed his toenails, rubbing tanning oil onto his face. "The sun burns me like the devil," he told the cop. "Fries me like an egg. Have some," he said, spritzing the cop with coconut oil. It wasn't the first time he'd shoplifted, and it wasn't the first time he'd gotten into trouble. To make a long story short, he's serving three and a half months.

"Here's the thing," Gus says, standing up. "We can't worry what other people think and we can't fix other people's problems. All we can do is take care of ourselves." Gus goes to the blackboard and writes the word *FEAR* in big letters. "Your dad passes out down the bay, and you're afraid. Afraid what the neighbors will think, afraid what will happen to him. But *fear* is really an

opportunity for you to"—and he points to each letter—
"Face Everything And Recover.

"Face Everything," he says, pointing to the *F* and the
E. "Face facts: your dad is drunk and he's passed out in
the sand. Fact: you can't stop him from drinking, even if
you drag him home in the wheelbarrow. Fact: you may
actually be preventing him from getting better because
you're not giving him the opportunity to wake up with
an earful of sand with the neighbors gawking out their
windows at him. You're protecting him from feeling
guilty or stupid or embarrassed."

All of us are looking at Gus like he's nuts.

"Do nothing?" the girl with the nose ring asks. "Like,
nothing?"

"Right. 'Cause you're not helping the situation.
You're trying to cover it up, and covering it up will only
keep your dad sick."

But if you do nothing, then nothing will change, I want
to say. The words are in my mouth, but they won't
come out.

"You can feel *fear*," Gus says, pointing to the letters.
"Or you can start to Face Everything And Recover."

"Or," Skate says, pointing to the letters, "Frig Everything And Run."

Everyone in the room laughs, even Gus and Nick.

"You definitely could," Gus says. "But is that going
to help? Think about it. What are you afraid of, Skate?"

"To tell the truth, fear isn't my problem," she says,

giving Gus a bored little smile. "I've got other things on my mind, but not that."

We wait for her to say more, but she doesn't.

Like what, Skate? I want to whisper.

"Ai-yi-yi," Skate says as we leave. She holds the door for me as I walk my bike out. "Drama Queen really pains my butt."

"Gus is nice, don't you think?" I ask.

"He's okay, but I wish he'd do something about those pimples." Even though it's stopped raining, heavy clouds hang in the sky. "I have money," she says. "Let's get pancakes."

I walk my bike through puddles and Skate slowly rides her board, and we make our way to Carolanne's on Pelican Drive. It's a tiny diner with a brightly lit clamshell on top. A long-haired mermaid peers over the top of the shell; she reminds me a little bit of Skate. We step inside and we're the only ones there, except for the waitress, Jeannie something, who goes to our school. Her bright blond hair is pulled back into a sleek ponytail. She's eating fries and has her nose in a Spanish III book.

We order one plate of chocolate chip pancakes with whipped cream, and two waters.

"So, hi, stranger," Skate says, resting her chin on her hands and staring at me. Skate and Dad both have bright blue eyes—eyes the color of island water—so blue you half expect to see tropical fish swimming there. Me, I have dark blue eyes—like my mom had, my dad used to tell me—eyes the color of the ocean on a cloudy day. We never knew our mom; she died when we were really little.

"Hi yourself, stranger," I say. Skate has been living with Julia, her boyfriend Perry's mom. Perry started college this fall at Rutgers. But even before our dad went to jail, Skate spent most of her time with Perry and his mom. I mostly see Skate at Heights—Ocean Heights High School—where she's a junior and I'm a sophomore.

"How's it going at home? How's what's-her-face?" Skate asks.

"*Angie*. She's nice. You should come over and visit." Our cousin Angie moved up from Florida to stay with us—well, me—when Dad went to jail. We were kids the last time we saw her. Angie's dad—our uncle Oscar—is the one footing our bills these days.

Jeannie brings our pancakes and says "Here you go" in a fakey-friendly voice, and that's when I know she *knows*. Or maybe I'm just imagining it. Skate says Little Mermaid is a small, mean town. I smile at Jeannie, but she's fake-smiling at the checkered tablecloth. Skate isn't looking, so she doesn't notice.

"Thanks," Skate says, lifting her fork and digging in.

"Listen," I whisper when Jeannie walks away. "Come with me on Saturday. To see Dad." I don't breathe, as if not breathing will keep her from saying no. She hasn't said yes yet.

"I'll see the Old Crow when he gets out," Skate says, sticking a forkful of whipped-cream-topped pancake into her mouth.

"It'll be months, Skate."

"Let him stew," she says. "Let him think about the mess he's made." She wraps her hair around her fist and flips it over her shoulder. "He stole your summer job money, for freak's sake!"

I feel Jeannie's eyes on us. Skate does too, and glares at Jeannie until she starts fidgeting with her earring and moves into the kitchen.

"Does everyone know?" I ask.

"Probably. She can kiss my butt."

I rest my head on my arms and smile at Skate. With her I never feel as afraid as I do alone in my room in the house. I wish she'd move back home. I wish I could be with her on nights when the ocean wind whistles and howls through the third floor and the floorboards creak and the house feels absolutely alive. Some nights, when there's enough moonlight, I can see the ocean from my window. Wave after wave crashes foamy to the shore. That's when my heart pounds and I feel afraid. When I'm afraid, I wish for so many things. I want my dad back. I want him well. I want Skate to forgive him. I want to love my friends (once I have some) and to kiss a boy (when I meet a good one). I want to have hope. And I do. Isn't it funny to have hope when everything feels broken? Here's another funny, secret thing: I'm glad my father is in jail. Because in jail he can't drink. He can't get into any more trouble. He'd been soggy with Old Crow whiskey for so long—so soggy his insides must have squished like a wet sponge—but now he's drying out. Everything has to change. I can feel it. This is what I want to tell Skate, but she won't believe me.

"He didn't steal," I say. "He'll pay me back when—"

"Rosie!" Skate says, reaching across the table and grabbing my wrist.

"What?"

"Snap out it! Don't be some dumb-ass girl with her head up her butt! *Dad* is a drunk and a shoplifter and a low-down thief who took three hundred bucks out of your sock drawer. That's who he is, the Old Crow. I told you, you should have opened a bank account. Julia would have cosigned for you. I told you."

"But he's sick, Skate. I mean, isn't he?"

"Well," Skate says, wadding up her napkin and dropping it onto the table. "Isn't it about time he got well?"

"He will. He is."

She stares at me.

"Can't you come visit him on Saturday? Just for a little while."

"You know that Perry's coming down for the

weekend." She swipes her finger through the whipped cream and takes a lick.

"You miss Perry?" I ask.

"You have no idea."

"What's it like, Skate?"

"What's what like?"

"Nothing," I say, feeling my face get hot.

"Hey, you're wearing mascara," she says, narrowing her eyes. "I knew something was different."

"Maybelline Great Lash."

"You like someone, don't you?"

"Not really," I say, and it's mostly true.

Skate waits for me to say more, and when I don't she says, "The girl with a million secrets. It's not Gus, I hope."

"Why?"

"Number one, he's too old for you. He's, like, twenty-two. Number two, he's too intense, too sad, too into the whole Drama Queen thing. I mean, can you imagine the guy having *fun*? *Please*. Number three . . . Well, I can't think of a number three."

"I know he's too old for me."

"He probably dates pimply college girls."

"You're terrible, Skate."

She puts her elbows on the table and cups her chin in her hands. "I speak the truth."

"Not everyone can look like Perry," I say. Skate is beautiful too. Her dark hair falls to her butt and the ends curl up in the salty sea air and she doesn't wear makeup, only lip gloss and funky nail polish. She wears holey cashmere sweaters from thrift shops, fringy tops, and her black Keds sneakers. She's not a girly girl. Neither am I. But guys stare at her. I don't wish for that, guys staring all the time. But still.

Skates plucks an ice cube from her glass. "What did you mean when you said 'What's it like?' Do you mean being in love? Being naked with a boy?"

"I don't know." I look down at the table and fork up a chocolate chip. When I look up Skate smiles at me and looks out the window, like she's thinking, but I can tell she's not thinking about me. "Please tell me you'll visit Dad sometime soon."

Skate sighs. "Rosie, please . . . Don't pain my butt." She signals Jeannie for the check and fishes in her pocket for money.

"Listen. Will you write him a letter?" I dig in my backpack for his address and rip out a sheet of paper and hand it to her. "Just a letter. Just a short note."

"Look, okay. I'll write to the Old Crow. Just don't be asking me when."

"And stop calling him the Old Crow."

But Skate is already heading for the door. Outside, it's drizzling, and I wipe beads of water off my bike seat. Skate flips her board onto the road and puts a foot on it. She tugs on a strand of my hair. "See ya, Great Lash."

"Come over soon, won't you? To visit me and Angie."

She shrugs. "Yeah, okay." Skate takes off, then makes a U-turn and pulls up next to me. "Rosie, you want to know what it's *like*? It's better than anything you know." She looks wickedly happy, and then with a few fast pushes she's off and zooming, her hair whipping out behind her. Even when I pick up some speed on my bike I won't be able to catch up.

Skate

Sometimes you gotta do what you gotta do. So on Friday I cut out of school before American lit. I forge a note from Angie, who's technically my guardian these days, saying I have a doctor's appointment. In my backpack I have a few books, lip gloss, underwear, a toothbrush, and a slice of Julia's homemade apple pie in plastic wrap. I get on my board and head to Sea Cove under a gloomy sky. I have to wait there for the train, then take the long ride up to Rutgers. I'm going to surprise Perry.

Last night he called and said, "Bad news, Skate." Before I could wrap my brain around that, he was telling me he couldn't come home this weekend and rattling off a list of stuff he had to do: a wicked-ass economics paper and studying for chemistry and calc tests. He said, "Next weekend, Skate. Next weekend is ours. Who loves you like a crazy man?" He always tells me he loves me like a crazy man.

So if he can't come to me, I'll go to him. I didn't call.

Didn't give him a chance to talk me out of it. I know he needs to study, so I'll only spend the night and scoot. I left a note for Julia this morning, telling her I have plans with Rosie tonight, then I grabbed Rosie coming out of assembly and told her my scheme, in case Julia's looking for me. "You can't," Rosie said, digging her fingers into my arm. "What if Julia calls the house?"

"She won't." But Rosie stood there chewing her lip, looking all worried. "Please don't pain my butt," I told her. "I *have* to go." Finally, she said okay.

Once I get to New Brunswick, I know my way. Perry and I made this trip together a couple of times over the summer. Some of the streets are hilly, too hilly to ride my board, so I walk part of the way as the sky darkens into a cool purple night. Dead leaves swirl above the sidewalk in little gusts, and then I'm standing in front of Perry's dorm. The place is swarming with kids talking and laughing, some on cell phones. "Eight o'clock. Squibley's," someone yells. Two laughing girls walk by holding witches' hats; Halloween is soon.

Perry lives on the ground floor, and I go inside as a couple of guys come out. Perry's room is at the end of the hall and the door is locked, so I tap a few times and wait. On his message board it says:

P—

SPARE SOME TIDE FOR A GUY WITH SMELLY SOCKS?
MOM-STER BOX DUE ANY DAY.
—G

I plop down on a beanbag chair in the common area to wait. He's bound to come sooner or later. I read a chapter in *The Scarlet Letter* as kids come in and out. A very blond girl smiles at me and I ask, "Do you know Perry Brockner?"

"Definitely," she says, coming over to me. "We have chem lab together." Her very blond hair is held back with a plaid headband. She even has blond eyelashes. She's as plain as a potato but seems nice.

"I'm his girlfriend," I say. "I'm waiting—"

"You must be Skate!" she says. "It's really nice to meet you. I'm Eleanor. You called his cell?"

I nod. I don't want her to know I don't have a cell. "I'm just waiting," I say.

"I'm upstairs, two-ten. If you need anything." She adjusts her plaid headband, smiles again, and heads out.

I make a list:

1. Cell phone

In the bottom of my backpack there's a bottle of nail polish, so I scrape off the sheer purple I'm wearing and put on a coat of sheer blue. Each time someone comes in, I snap my head up, but it's not Perry. A cute boy smiles at me and I smile back. This other guy walks back and forth, checking me out. "Hey," he finally says. I smile, blow on a nail.

I imagine talking to these boys, telling them my name is Skate. *Skate.* For the first time it sounds a little freaky to me. I've been called Skate since I learned to ride a board at five. I was good at it, right from the get-go. I could do a hardflip and a grind by the time I was seven. "Skate" stuck. And my board still gets me around, of course. But it might be nice to have a car. *Car,* I add to my list.

Perry has Julia's old Hyundai. But me get a car? Not likely, considering the Old Crow doesn't even have *his* anymore. He totaled his pickup a couple of months before he went to jail. He was fined and sent to rehab, and the same day he got out of rehab, the *same day,* he started drinking again, even though Rosie and I had found every hidden bottle of whiskey and dumped them down the drain while he was gone.

The last time I saw the Old Crow drive was right before he rammed into the seawall. There he was, creeping down Ocean Avenue, barely doing the speed limit. I was on my board, coming in the opposite direc-tion. He was spaced-out, hunched over the wheel like an old lady, talking to himself, or singing. I don't know. I was on my board heading toward him—there was just me and him, no other cars or people, and he looked at me but didn't even see me. *Me,* Skate. He was just all wasted in his Old Crow fog. So I flipped him the bird. Still nothing. Jesus. I get hot and bothered remembering that, so I take off my sweater and stuff it in my backpack.

Maybe it's time to ditch "Skate." My real name is Olivia. Maybe I could go by Liv, like Liv Tyler. Or Via might work. I wonder if I look like a Via. I take out a pocket mirror and have a look. "Via," I say. Nope. Not seeing it.

Still no Perry. I get a drink from the water fountain, and after, while I'm digging in my backpack for a half-eaten bag of pretzels, I find the scrap with the Old Crow's address. There it is in Rosie's small, neat print: *inmate number 147782*. How did the Old Crow become 147782? How does that happen to a person? I wad it up and toss it into the trash.

Oh, Perry, where are you? I miss him every which way. Home just isn't the same without him—Little Mermaid is now like a shell without the roar of the ocean. He's my best friend. He never lies to me. If I had a snot hanging in my nose, he'd tell me. We used to spend every single day together, so I miss everything. Surfing, hanging out, eating pepperoni calzones at Denardino's on the boardwalk, crabbing with drop lines in the lagoon, running into each other between classes, getting naked, kissing, holding hands, sex picnics. But I really miss talking. My talk time has been cut in half. So I wait for the weekends that Perry can come home. During the week we only talk for minutes at a time because Perry's always coming or going. So I leave him long messages on his cell. I tell him what I'm thinking. I talk about all kinds of things, the Old Crow and everything. Half a conversation is better than no conversation; at least it's something until we can see each other.

Julia says I need some girlfriends. But that's because

she has a slew of girlfriends. She's divorced from Perry's dad and she dates this guy named Hal, but she's always going out with her girls. I'm friendly with a lot of kids at school, but there's no one I like as much as Perry.

Then, as if he's heard me, he comes through the door. "Perry!" I say. He's with a girl, a girl with dark gleaming hair and dark eyes like his. "Skate!" he says, stopping and staring at me in wonder. He hugs me tight.

"This is Gina. We've been studying." Gina and I smile at each other. Her hair shines under the lights.

"So, we can finish up over the weekend, then," Gina tells Perry. "We have a big test next week," she says to me. She ducks out the door into the raindrops, waving goodbye.

"Well, look at you," Perry says. He wraps an arm around me and plants a little kiss on my forehead.

"You can do better than that, mister," I say.

"All in good time, pal," he says. "So, what the heck, Skate?"

"We need a night, me and you."

He smiles and nods and gently takes my fingers and leads me down the hall. He laughs when he reads his message board. Inside, he puts my backpack on his chair and kisses me, a real kiss. We tumble onto the bed and cuddle for a while. I tell him my scheme, how glad I am to be here, how long I've been sitting on the beanbag waiting. "I'm starving," I say, touching his face. "Let's go get pizza or something." Raindrops hit the windows.

"I've got a better idea. Simon went home, so we've got the room to ourselves." He takes out his laundry detergent. "Be right back," he says.

I hear him knocking on doors and soon he returns with a wedge of cheddar cheese, a chocolate Pop-Tart, and a big fat tomato. "Dragonetti's mom grows them in her garden. We're going to have a feast." He gets out a hot pot, a toaster, a can of soup, and a couple of English muffins from the minifridge. He gets the soup going, toasts the muffins, and slices the cheese and tomato on his desk. The rain is coming down harder, spraying the outside windows. Perry closes the drapes, lights a candle, and puts on *Drops of Jupiter.* We sit cross-legged on the floor smiling at each other. He toasts the muffins again, this time with cheese and tomato, as the soup bubbles in the pot. And then Perry hands me a Tupperware bowl of Chicken with Stars and a bent spoon. I will always remember this. My dinner feast in Perry's dorm.

We eat all of it, and I pull out Julia's pie. "Smell that," I say. "Your mom and her girlfriends went apple picking this week." The pie's for Perry, but he keeps giving me bites, 'cause he's nice like that. We lick our fingers and mop up every last crumb from the plastic. We decide, though, to save the Pop-Tart for breakfast.

We climb under the covers while the rain batters the windows. Perry pulls off his sweatshirt and I touch the tattoo of a vine that laces around his upper arm. I want one too. Someday. In my mind I write it on my list under cell phone and car: *vine tattoo.*

We kiss for a long time. "I miss you," I say.

"This is hard, isn't it?" I nod and he holds me tight. His cell phone rings.

"Please don't get it."

"No," he says.

We kiss some more and Perry pulls away and looks at me. "But, Skate, you shouldn't worry my mom."

"I'm not. Jesus, Perry. Why do you say that?"

"What if she calls over to your house? Huh?"

"She won't. Besides, Rosie knows. Rosie's on it. Relax."

"Rosie the accomplice," he says, and snorts. "Rosie's a terrible liar."

"What's eating you? Jesus. Aren't you happy to see me?"

"Yes," he says, burying his face against me. I can feel him smile against my neck. "I'm very happy."

"Good," I say. "Then shut up."

"And another thing."

"Oh, for freak's sake."

He props himself up on one elbow and looks down at me. "You have to visit your dad."

"That's it," I say, throwing off the covers and swinging my legs out of bed.

He grabs my arm and pulls me back. "Listen to me,

you old hothead. Your dad is a fact of your life, sorry-ass that he is."

Perry's own dad is a bit of a sorry-ass too. He cheated on Julia more than once, but he mostly makes his child-support payments and he's forked over some tuition money, so he's not a deadbeat. I plop back down on the pillow and Perry covers me with the blanket.

"Whose side are you on?" I ask.

"Yours."

I cup his face with my hands and look at him, so that he really *sees* me. "He's a screwup, Perry. He's a loser. I can't bear him."

"You don't have to bear him. Visit him for an hour. I'll come, if you want."

"How about a letter. I'll write him."

"A letter's good."

"Okay. Now will you shut up?" Tomorrow I'll have to remember to fish his address out of the garbage. Not that I'm in any hurry to write him.

Perry curls around me. "Now I'll shut up, but you have to leave in the morning. I swear. I'm drowning here." I look over at the stack of books.

"What time you throwing me out?"

"After the Pop-Tart. I'll walk you to the train and then head over to the library." On his nightstand he has a picture of us holding hands in our wet suits on the beach. Our hair is dripping.

"Next weekend. Next weekend is ours," I say, looking into his eyes.

"Yes, yes, yes," Perry whispers, kissing my forehead, nose, and mouth.

He turns off the lamp, and the candle flickers. "I like college," I say.

"Good." He laughs. "At least one of us does."

"I met Eleanor. She's really friendly."

"Did you? Elle's great. She's my chem partner. She's much smarter than me."

"And the other girl?"

"Gina? We've got economics together."

"Gina's awfully pretty, dude."

"So?" he says, looking at me dreamy.

"So nothing." He kisses me.

"Tell me something," I say, brushing my hair out of my face. "Do I look like a Liv?"

He shakes his head and pulls my T-shirt over my head. "An Olivia?"

"You're Skate. It's perfectly you." I pull his shirt off. "I love you like a crazy man," he whispers, gathering me half-naked in his arms. He's back, my crazy man.

Rosie

Ocean Grove Correctional Facility could be worse, but still, it's pretty bad. As I move up to the second checkpoint, a beefy guard roots around in my pocketbook with his hairy arm. I won't look at him.

We move quickly into the visitors' room and I grab Monopoly off the shelf. First time here I learned two things. First, you've got to get here early if you want a game—Monopoly, Scrabble, Yahtzee, Rummikub—all go fast. Second, you need quarters for the vending machine if you want to eat. A frozen pizza is three dollars—twelve quarters—and there are no change machines. You can't leave to get quarters and then come back. Once you leave for the day, the guards won't let you back in.

It's a big ugly gray room with long tables and benches. With quarters in my pocket, I sit with Angie at one of the center tables, clutching the Monopoly game. We wait. Angie blows a small pink bubble, sucks it back into her mouth, and smiles at me. She's a hairstylist and recently got a job at the one salon on the island. She has a Cleopatra hairdo that she dyes black. It's blunt cut at chin level, with dark bangs that almost touch her eyelashes. She's pretty, but a little on the chubby side. I wonder if she's mad about last night. It's a long story, but the short version is that Angie figured out Skate forged her name on the note for school, and Julia knows Skate went to Rutgers. Skate sure can cause trouble.

Finally, a guard opens the door, and the men come in wearing orange jumpsuits, looking like construction workers. I wonder what their crimes are. My dad walks a little stiffly, like he has old-man legs. "Hello, my loves," he says, easing himself onto the bench. Boy, does he look bad, like a deflated balloon, but his eyes are bright and blue. I feel nervous, fluttery, the way I do every week, as if I'm meeting somebody new.

"I'll be the shoe," Dad says. He flicks the piece over to GO, next to my top hat. Then he hunches over and watches me set up the board. I separate the greasy property cards and count out our stacks of money. He's still got the shakes, but only a little bit.

"I'm going to buy up everything I land on, even the cheapies," I tell him. "I'm going to be a slumlord."

"Okay, Slummy," he says. "Roll." Angie doesn't want to play, so she sits nearby flipping through *Rolling Stone*.

I roll, land on Community Chest and have to pay

forty dollars for opera lessons. Then he rolls and is fined a hundred dollars for parking. I sneak a look at him—at his tiny, hairy wrists and his skinny neck. I wonder if his brain is still soggy with Old Crow or if he's drying out. This morning as I brushed my teeth I decided I would call a duck a duck. Gus at the meetings is always saying, "Tell the truth, tell it like it is." He says, "If it quacks like a duck and it looks like a duck, then it's a duck." Once, Nick, the guy from my homeroom, the guy with the dad in the sand, said, "I don't have any problem calling a duck a duck. I just don't know what to do about the *duck*."

I roll the dice and say, "Dad, you look crappy."

"I feel crappy, love."

Oh, Dad! My heart rattles my ribs. "You don't look so bad," I lie.

"I do so," he says, sliding his eyes to me. "Listen, love, my crappiness has nothing to do with you." But why does this make me feel crappier? We take turns rolling the dice. We both collect some property. I wonder if either of us will land in jail.

A spiky-haired kid sits nearby, boring his eyes into my skull. "When will you be done?"

"I don't know. A little while," I say.

"Billy!" the kid's mother yells. "Stop bothering the girl. Come play Clue with your sister."

"I hate Clue. It bites. The stupid colonel did it with

the stupid wrench in the stupid kitchen." He glares at me, looks down at the Monopoly board, and slinks away.

"Rosie, love," Dad whispers. "What do you say we let the kid play?"

"Don't you want to play?"

"I don't give a rat's behind about Monopoly. I'm just happy to see you," he says, reaching across the table and squeezing my hand. His fingers are warm and shaky.

I know I should let the boy have the game. He's just a kid, maybe ten. But for some reason I don't understand, I really want to play Monopoly with my dad. I look across the table at him.

"Okay, then. Roll, Slummy."

I do.

We play for a little longer, but after a while my heart isn't in it either. "We can stop," I say. Dad nods and yawns. I start picking up the pieces.

The kid pushes up next to me. "Let me do it!" He lines up the box with the table and with one sweep of his arm, the cards, playing pieces, dice, houses, and hotels land in the box. "You're a real ball breaker," he says to me, and turns away.

Dad lets out a loud whoop. It's been so long since I heard him laugh like that. "You should meet her sister," he says. We smile at each other, a real smile. "No Skate today?"

I shake my head.

He nods. "Maybe one of these weeks."

"Maybe," I say, nodding hopefully.

"I bet she's fuming at me."

"I don't know," I lie.

"We'll work it out," he says, winking. "She still work on Saturdays at the fish market?"

"Dad, that was two years ago! Skate works on the boardwalk."

"I've got scrambled eggs up here," he says, knocking on his head.

I tell him about Lucky Louie's, the arcade Skate works at. Mostly she works the prize counter. You win tickets playing Skee-Ball and other games and then cash them in for stuff like yo-yos, spider rings, and Super-Balls. Junk, Skate calls it. The good stuff, the ministereo and food processor, is like 130,000 points. No one ever cashes in enough tickets. When the fortune-teller machine doesn't spit out a fortune she'll give it a good kick. She does just about everything.

"And you?"

"You remember my summer job?" I ask.

"Down the bay . . . ," he says, gesturing with his thumb. "Yeah, at, um . . ."

So I tell him how I worked at Barnacle Bob's—the bike and raft rental and the candy counter. I'll work there again next summer.

"I remember," he says, but I don't believe him.

I look into his eyes, wondering if he remembers taking my money out of my drawer. Money I made blowing up dragon rafts, scooping Italian ice, and selling taffy. I stand and dig into my pocket. "I'm going to get a pizza."

"I got a couple bucks," Dad says, reaching for his pocket.

"You need quarters, Dad." I head over to the vending machine and slide in all my quarters and a frozen pizza lands with a satisfying bang.

I get in the microwave line. Two people are in front of me, a drippy-nosed kid with mozzarella sticks and an orange-suited guy with a bean burrito. The guy could be, say, my geometry teacher. He has short hair and a bit of a gut. What could he have done? Tax evasion, I decide. A skinny guy built like a whooping crane buys a root beer and sits down with an older couple. His parents, I think. Maybe a cat burglar. A tattooed guy with a ponytail holds a baby—credit-card theft. Even a little kid looks guilty, dragging his dirty blanket. Maybe if you could look into everyone's heart you'd see a crime. What's mine? Can't call a duck a duck.

I have to wait three minutes for the mozzarella sticks and another four minutes for the burrito. I keep looking back at my dad, like he might disappear. He and Angie are talking, and I wonder if she'll tell him about Skate cutting school and going to Rutgers. Not that it matters, because what can he do, but I don't think she will. Finally, I pop my pizza in the microwave. Three minutes later it's steaming and smelling good. I grab napkins.

"Have some," I tell Dad.

He shakes his head.

"Angie, eat," I say.

"Not after that breakfast we had. I'm having salad for the rest of the day."

"Eat!" I push the plate toward my dad.

"Bossy," he says, taking a mouse-sized bite and then pushing the plate back at me. "Is it good to be back in the Garden State, Angie?"

"God, yes. Miami was fun, but it's such a scene. Everyone's so skinny and tan and fabulous. I just want to wear a winter coat and eat Oreos." Dad smiles. "I love the old house, and Rosie and I are hitting it off."

Dad gives me a little kick under the table. "She's a good kid, this one."

"I've been meaning to ask," Angie says, fidgeting. "I mean, is it okay that Skate stays with her boyfriend's mom? I mean, it's fine, right?" Angie keeps smoothing her skirt, which is a little too tight. Skate would probably say she looks stuffed into it, like a sausage.

Dad looks at me, and I see he has no idea what's going on.

"She's been at Julia's for a while now," I tell him. "Even before you came here. She spent a lot of time there."

He nods, but I don't think he's getting it.

"Perry's at Rutgers," I say louder. "He started in September."

He nods again. No idea, he has no idea.

"So that's fine?" Angie asks him.

"It's okay with—" Dad looks at me helplessly.

"Julia!" I snap. "Julia is Perry's mom."

Dad nods and covers my hand with his, but I slide my hand away.

"What's it like in here?" I blurt out.

"There are a lot of rules."

"What kind of rules?"

"When to get up, when to shower, when to eat." He sighs. "When to talk, when to be quiet, when to go to bed."

"Is it terrible?"

"Nah," he says. "There aren't any bad characters in here."

"What's your room like?"

"A dormitory."

"What's that like? I want to picture it."

"No, you don't, honey."

"I do."

He explains to me. It's a very large room with windows. There are about forty bunk beds. He has a bottom bunk. Every bed has a pillow and a blanket. Sheets and pillowcases are changed every week.

"Do you have a closet? Drawers?"

"A small locker." He sighs again. "You're wearing me out, kid."

"What do you have in your locker?"

He gives me the list: his toothbrush, razor, and bath things. He has three orange jumpsuits, underwear, and socks. Also a picture of me and Skate and my mom on the beach, sitting on a blanket eating sandwiches. I don't remember this one.

"Do you get sunshine in the dorm?"

"In the morning."

"What time do they make you get up?"

"Six-thirty."

"Where's the bathroom?"

"Right next door."

"Do you have to wait in line?"

"It's a big room. Rosie, you're wearing me out."

"Wait, you mean a big room with showers and toilet stalls? Like a gym?"

"Yup, but no stalls."

"No stalls at all?"

"We don't have any privacy, love."

"You have to go the bathroom in front of everybody?"

He nods. "That's jail, love."

"You mean," I whisper, "you have to use the toilet in front of everyone?"

"That's the way it works."

How awful that is, maybe more awful than being locked up. I start to cry. I try not to, but I feel my eyes fill and spill over. How can you not have privacy when sitting on the toilet? He takes my hand again and I let him. "You're a funny kid," he says. "Don't think about it."

I'm really crying now and I don't have a tissue, so I wipe my nose on my sleeve. Angie roots around in her bag and finds one, all crumpled, with lint stuck to it. I don't care and blow my nose loudly. Who's going to like a girl like me, a girl with a dad in jail? When am I going to be kissed? Probably never. I close my eyes and sink into tears.

"It's not meant to be a picnic, love," Dad says gently. He is calm and holding my hand. His hand shakes like it has a little heartbeat all its own.

I open my eyes and look out the dirty window to the stream of sunlight in the fenced yard. I stop crying. "You have eleven weeks and two days left."

"I can do it." He waves his fist in the air, a little victory cheer.

"Look, the sun," Angie says. We walk over to the windows. Outside there's a courtyard. It's nothing much, concrete and some benches surrounded by a fence. But it's enough to walk around and you can tip your face up to the sky. A lone dandelion pops through a patch of dirt between the concrete slabs.

"Let's take a little walk," Dad says, slinging an arm over my shoulder.

Angie pulls her Jetta into the driveway, turns off the motor, and says, "Screw the salad. Let's have tacos. You need some tacos, Rosie."

I smile because I know Angie really wants tacos, but they sound good to me too.

"I'll go to A&P and be back in a jiff." As I open my door, she says, "You know, Rosie, you can invite a friend over. It's cool."

"I don't really have friends," I say. Angie looks down at the steering wheel, embarrassed for me, I think, so I tell her about Carrie Barnes, who was my best friend in elementary up through eighth grade, but then her dad got a job in Illinois and they moved. "Guess I haven't replaced her yet."

"Well, maybe you will. Okay, scoot. Let me get us some taco fixings."

I let myself in the side door and attack the kitchen. We were running late this morning and left all the breakfast dishes, and the hot chocolate has a funky skin on top and the goo on the egg plates has hardened.

I guess it's weird that I haven't made friends since Carrie moved away. But it's not like I'd ever want to invite anyone over with my dad drunk on the couch.

I've just gotten a sinkful of sudsy hot water going

when Skate walks in the side door and slides into a kitchen chair. "I had," she gushes, "an *excellent* time."

I turn to face her and drip water on the floor. "Julia knows you went to Rutgers and Angie knows you faked her name on the note."

"Crap! How did *that* happen?"

I slide the egg plate back into the water and tell her the story. The school called and left a message to confirm that Skate had a doctor's appointment.

"Did she?" Angie asked when I got home.

"Maybe," I said, turning red, but I don't tell Skate that part. Then, wouldn't you know that when we went to Denardino's for subs and salad, we ran into Julia and her boyfriend, who came in for pizza.

Julia said, "Oh, I thought Skate was with you?" and I had to shrug, but I don't tell Skate this part either. And that was when Angie asked Julia if Skate had to leave school early for a doctor's appointment. Catching on, Julia made a face.

"She forged my name," Angie said, trying not to smile.

"I bet she went to Rutgers," Julia said, not smiling at all. Busted in less than ten seconds.

"Oh, crap!" Skate says. "Is Angie here?"

"She went to get taco makings. She'll be back."

Skate sighs. "Crap . . ."

I turn back to the dishes. What Skate doesn't get is

that if she had come with me to see Dad none of this would have happened.

"You should have said I was at work or something," Skate says. I twist around in time to see her stick her elbow in some maple syrup. She makes a face. "God, the two of you are slobs. Throw me that sponge. Frank totally would have covered for me if they called over to Lucky's."

"Why didn't you tell me that?" I throw the sudsy sponge and it ricochets wet off her sweatshirt. Doesn't Skate know I don't want to lie for her?

"Don't give me that look," Skate says. "Is Julia pissed?"

"More worried, I think. She was going to call Perry's last night. Didn't he get the call?"

Skate shakes her head.

"You know, you could take off before Angie gets back," I say, wondering if Angie's mad. I'm not in the mood for a fight.

"I'm not going anywhere," Skate says, unzipping her sweatshirt. "Besides, I could eat again. I had a chicken pot pie, but that was just a snack."

"Aren't you going to ask how Dad is?"

"So, tell me."

"He's okay, Skate. He asked about you. You'll, um, write to him, won't you?"

"Here we go again," Skate groans. "By the way, I lost his address."

"I'll get it for you." I sigh and slip into a chair beside her. "Why do I feel so crappy?"

"Well, it's an all-around crappy situation. The Old Crow . . . ," Skate says, shaking her head, as if he's the only problem.

"So was it nice to see Perry?"

Skate closes her eyes for a second. "Yes!" she whispers, and her face turns all rosy.

When Angie gets back, she doesn't mention the note or Rutgers or anything about it. Soon we're all working. Skate shreds the cheese, and I chop up a tomato and an avocado. Angie browns the meat and it sizzles in the pan. We get dinner going and then sit down to eat.

"I remember when you were a goth," Skate says to Angie, biting into her taco.

"A lovely ghoul, wasn't I?" Angie says.

"Skate and I thought you must love Halloween," I pipe up. Angie must have been our age at the time, maybe a little older, like seventeen. Skate and I were just little kids. Angie wore all black with really pale makeup. Eyes ringed in black, black lipstick. Black hair teased high.

"How'd you get your hair to do that?" Skate asks.

"Egg whites. You beat them in a bowl until they stiffen into peaks and then apply the gloop to your hair." She laughs. "Oh, the things I could do! Horns. A modified Mohawk."

"Were you as scary as you looked?" I ask.

Angie shakes her head. "We mostly sat around diners eating French fries and talking about boys. I secretly loved disco. *'I need some hot stuff, baby, tonight,'* " she sings, pulsing her arm in the air.

We eat all the tacos and refried beans and toppings and then sit at the table looking at the mess. I want the dishes to float over to the sink and dip themselves in some soapy water.

"So, Skate . . . ," Angie says. Skate looks up at her. "So you're writing notes and signing my name and skipping out of school?"

"Yeah, I guess you could say that. Just once."

Angie sighs. "I did that once or twice myself." Then she sinks down in her chair and clasps her stomach. "Ugh. I feel like a pig."

"Me too," I say, unbuttoning my jeans.

"And I have to get up early to work." Angie yawns and rolls her eyes up to the clock.

Skate picks some cheese out of the bowl and nibbles it off her fingers. Then she stacks up some plates and bowls and heads over to the sink. "Look, Angie, I'm sorry," she says, turning on the water and squirting detergent.

"Okay, then," Angie says.

And it seems like that's that.

Skate

When I do my homework and Julia's cooking, she'll flip me a slice of cheese or tomato or a noodle because she knows how much I like to eat. But tonight she ignores my wiggling fingers when I hold out my hand for a slice of mozzarella.

"I have a buck." Fishing a dollar out of my pocket, I toss it on the countertop. "What'll that get me?" She doesn't smile. "I know you know," I say finally.

Julia sighs and puts down her knife. "Skate . . . ," she says. With the back of her hand she pushes hair off her face. She dyes her hair flaming red and twists it back with sparkly clips. But other than the movie-star hair, she's mostly an ordinary kind of mom. "You can't stay here if you lie to me."

"I needed to go, Julia."

"You need to go to school too, and you can't lie to me." She looks me dead in the eye. "You're sixteen years old. You're a minor. You're not even allowed in the dorm—"

"Oh, Julia, no one knew. And I skedaddled pretty early—"

"You can't lie to me!"

I don't know what to say, so I just say "I'm sorry."

She scoops homemade marinara sauce over the noodles and tops in off with a layer of cheese. Then she pops it into the oven and sets her lemon timer. "You know, Skate, it's going to be hard with Perry away at school now. Maybe you guys should cool it for a while. I'm not saying you can't be together, but maybe not as together . . ."

"Do you want me to leave?" I stand up. "Is that what you're saying?" I imagine hauling myself back to my wreck of a house.

"Cool your jets, kiddo," Julia says, placing her hand over mine. "That's not what I'm saying."

"Did Perry say we shouldn't be together?" I whisper.

She shakes her head. "I just mean he's *there.*" She points out the window, across the smooth surface of the lagoon. "And you're *here.*" She points firmly to the floor. "You're always waiting for him, to call, to come home. You need to have a life here, Skate, because this is where you are."

She flips me a scrap of mozzarella and I wolf it down. Julia's lemon timer is ticking away. I love that thing, like I love her house. It's quiet here. Her place is tiny compared to mine, but she has so many nice things, like the lemon timer and a cuckoo clock. On the hour a twittery bird pokes its head out and sings a few notes, its little neck moving back and forth; every hour, you can count on it. And Julia knows how to cook so many good things—cheesy, saucy, spicy things. And nothing here leaks, or falls apart, or gives you a splinter.

"You shouldn't act like I'm a kid, Julia. When Perry and I are together we're not sixteen and eighteen or anything. We're just us."

She smiles and rinses the cutting board.

"You get it, don't you?" I say.

She nods slowly, but she's thinking something, something she's not saying. "How is Perry?" she asks.

"Good. Really busy, but good. He's made a lot of friends. And, Julia, I'm doing fine in school. I'll probably get a couple of As and Bs this quarter." We stare at each other and I want to tell her how happy Perry was to see me, but I don't. "Everything's fine" is all I say.

"Okay then." Julia settles on the couch with the *Asbury Park Press*. I stand there for a second, looking at her, all comfy on the couch with her ankles crossed, her silvery ankle bracelet catching the light, and I feel sad for some reason, like something has changed, or will change, but that's not exactly right. Or is it? I need to get out of here for a while. I tell Julia I'm going to visit

Rosie, maybe eat dinner there, and she tells me to heat up some ziti if I want it when I come back.

I ride my board over to my house. You should see the old wreck. My great-grandfather built it in the 1930s. It's got three stories, wraparound porches and balconies, six bedrooms and a turret, like a castle. Once it was fit for a queen and the whole royal family, but it has dry rot, the roof is caving in, the staircases are splintery, the furnace conks out, and the third-floor ceiling leaks, so we have to line the rooms with buckets and pots and pans to collect the drips when it rains. It's still something, this huge old house by the sea, but mostly it's sad and decrepit. And we're no royal family. It's always been just me and Rosie and the Old Crow.

Inside, it smells good, like hamburgers and fried onions. The table is messy with books and crumbs and a damp towel. I open the refrigerator and find a bowl with mac 'n' cheese covered in plastic wrap. It's still warm and I finger some into my mouth. On the refrigerator door I see a little list that shocks me: *Chores,* it says. Angie's divvied up stuff like laundry, dusting and vacuuming, cooking. She even has me on there, next to *Cleaning 2nd floor bathroom.* That's the big bathroom with the claw-foot tub. And *Chores*—how do you like that word? It's right out of *Little House on the Prairie.* (*Hey, Pa, I'm going to do my chores. Okay, Half-pint.*)

I head upstairs, past the bathroom, where Angie is

on her knees, running water in the tub and scrubbing with a big brush. Funny thing—Angie likes wearing the color lemon-lime—picture Mountain Dew, antifreeze, baby puke. Listen, I'm no fashionista. I mean, I look *good*. I definitely do. But who looks good in lemon-lime? Who? And Angie's got a bit of an ass. So we're talking about a big lemon-lime ass.

I hang back, not wanting to get snagged into cleaning the bathroom. On the third floor I hear the vacuum. I sit on the stairs, trying to decide what to do. Rosie's playing the Stones upstairs. If I stay I'm going to be guilt-tripped into scrubbing the toilet or mopping a floor. Plus Rosie's going to get on me about writing a letter to the Old Crow. But I don't want to go back to Julia's just yet. I slide down the banister for old times' sake—heavy-duty jeans, no splinter worries. I scoop more macaroni into my mouth and then slip out the door. I walk onto the beach, onto a dune, and lie on my hood and make a sand angel. *And you're here*—I hear Julia's words again. The sun burns weakly behind the clouds and the wind makes me shiver. How am I going to get through this year without Perry?

"Hey, Frank, I'm going to hang out, if that's okay." Frank is my boss at Lucky Louie's on the boardwalk. He's sprawled out on the floor, fixing Skee-Ball lane number one.

"Hey, LD," he says. LD stands for *lovely dude,* which

is what he calls all the pretty girls. "I'm fixing this mother once and for all."

"Good luck," I tell him. Skee–Ball lane number one sticks. We have to walk up the alley to manually release the little gate nearly every time. Frank has a box of pepperoni, mushroom, and sausage pizza on the counter, and I bite into a slice.

"Help yourself to pizza," he yells.

"I already am, thanks," I say with my mouth full. "Can I use your cell?"

"Anything else?" He looks over and smirks.

"I'll make it snappy." I move to the other end of the arcade and dial Perry. It rings and rings. *And you're here.*

"You got me. I'll call you back," says Perry's voice mail. It's Sunday night. Where can he be? He's probably in the library and has his phone off.

"Hey, it's me," I say. "Well, I just wanted to say hi. I had such a good time Friday. Call me later. No, I'll call you." I munch on my slice and take the keys from behind the prize counter and turn on the fortune-teller machine. It's a booth with a gypsy-lady mannequin inside draped in flashy jewels and a turban. The lights blink and she passes her long fingers over a crystal ball. In a second a card shoots out. *You love high jinks and escapades.* I toss the card into my backpack on top of my underwear and toothbrush.

"Frank, can I come live with you?"

"Yow!" he says. "And what will I tell my girl-friends?"

"I just want to sleep on your couch, dude."

He sits up and smiles at me. Frank is cute, totally cute, and he's a big-ass flirt. He's twenty-one and works at the arcade year-round. His dad is Louie, Lucky Louie, and he and Frank's mom live most of the year in Florida. Frank takes one class a semester at Ocean County College, and sometimes he even drops the class. At this rate he figures he'll have a bachelor's in another ten years. He has lots of girlfriends and is always getting into trouble with them because he falls in and out of love really fast. He has a big friendly face and light brown wind-blown hair and green eyes the color of sea glass.

He puts down his wrench and walks over, grabs a slice and takes a gargantuan bite, and then chews like a mad-man. Cute, but a pig. As he chews he gives me the once-over. "Did you get thrown out of what's-her-name's?"

"Let's just say I pissed her off."

"So move back home."

"Unh-uh," I say, moving my tongue around my molars, trying to get out the stuck cheese. "My cousin's there and she's got this major cleaning campaign going, and, Frank, you know how freakin' big the house is."

"What a drag," Frank says, looking away. He knows about my dad, and whenever I mention anything about my, you know, *situation,* he gets kind of uneasy.

"Did you see Brockner?"

I tell him how I went up to Rutgers.

"So that's why his old lady is pissed." I nod. "Listen to Frankie," he says, clapping me on the back. "Lay low. Go home, scrub the sink. It'll blow over and then you can go back to whoosie's."

Maybe. But neither option sounds good to me. Frank goes back over to the Skee-Ball lane. I scrounge up a pen from the bottom of my backpack and write on the pizza box.

Hi Dad, hope you're okay. I know it must be pretty crappy and all but I hope you're getting through the days. And I seriously hope that we've seen the last of your drunken escapades. As I write this, I realize that's a big wish, one that might never come true. Sorry if that's harsh, but I'm not going to feed you some bull. Maybe the good thing to come out of all this is that I'm not much of a drinker. At parties I'll sip a beer but once I get a little warm glow going I stop. Lots of kids are sloppy stupid fools when they drink but I'm not. I think we can both feel good about that. Just so you *know—I'm okay and Perry is too. And Rosie is fine, but you probably already know that.*

I chew on the pen, thinking.

I hope you have some time for whatever good things jail might offer.

Take care,
Skate

Frank lets out a madman yell. "I'm going to have to completely take this mother apart. Completely!"

"Relax. Big whoop if we have to walk up the alley and release it manually."

"Lovely dude, listen to me," Frank says, waving his wrench and getting himself all worked up. "The balls should come rumbling down when you put in your quarter."

I shake my head. Such a perfectionist, that Frank. He sighs deeply and comes lugging over. I reread my letter, rip off the top of the pizza box, and stuff it in my backpack.

"Hey! I'm having those slices for breakfast and now it's all going to dry out." He's so close to me I can smell him, a warm, greasy but not un-nice smell.

"Have you heard of plastic wrap, Frank?"

"Shoot! I don't have plastic wrap."

"So go to the A&P."

"Now I've got to go to the A&P!" he says, throwing up his hands. "Man . . ."

"Sorry, Frank. I didn't have paper and needed to write something."

"The *scholar*," he says.

"Go to the A&P, it won't kill you," I say, zipping up my backpack.

"Go scrub a sink, it won't kill you."

I wave. "See you Thursday."

There aren't many people around in the off-season, and the stands on the boardwalk are mostly empty. I buy a piece of fudge at the sweet shop from Jill, a sleepy-looking girl with a flowered head scarf and big hoop earrings who's in my American lit class. While Jill gets my change, she fills me in on what I missed in class on *The Scarlet Letter.* "You could come over, Skate, and copy my notes. I'm outta here in, like, ten minutes." She reaches into the case and pops a chocolate cream into her mouth.

"Nah, I gotta bounce," I tell her. "But thanks. I'll copy them in class." I stand in the wind eating my fudge, my hair and fingers getting sticky with chocolate. Then I get on my board and ride. It's dark and the cold feels good on my face. I ride along the ocean and take the cutoff for the bay, toward Julia's. But with the wind whipping at me, biting me, I slow down and stop, blinking up at the streetlights.

I don't want to go to Julia's. I *would* lie to her again. If it meant another night with Perry, getting to be with him, I'd definitely lie to her. I'd do whatever it took, even though I like Julia so much.

So I turn down my street, ride up to the wreck, and slip in through the side door. I hear the TV on in the family room and see the backs of Angie's and Rosie's heads—those old clean freaks—and sneak up the back stairway to my old room. I'll call Julia and tell her I'm spending the night—after I call Perry again.

Rosie

In between geometry proofs I braid tiny sections of my hair. I've got about eight minibraids finished off in tiny blue and gold elastics when Angie yells up the stairs, "Rosie, phone." I hurry downstairs wondering if it's Skate. She's been sleeping here the past few nights, but she comes in late and leaves early, so I haven't seen much of her.

"A boy," Angie mouths, handing me the phone. *Gus!*

"Hello," I say, my heart thumping in my ears.

"Rosie? This is Nick from, you know, the meetings. Listen, could I ask you a favor? . . . Can you meet me at the bay off Cove Road? Is that okay?"

"Oh," I say, fingering my braids. "Do you mean now?"

"If you can't—"

"I can. I'll come."

I sort of don't want to go because I was hoping Skate might show up early tonight. But I put on my jean jacket and wrap a furry purple scarf around my neck. Tonight you can feel the nip of winter in the air. I get on my bike and ride the streets to Cove Road, a secret part of the bay hidden in tall cattails. Somehow I know I'm going to see Nick's drunk father.

Nick is sitting on the dock holding a blanket and a pillow, and his dad is passed out on the sand. Flat on his back. The wind ripples the surface of the bay. "Hey," Nick says, lifting his head.

The dock is old and rotten and lumpy under my butt. I stretch out my legs in front of me and look down at them. I don't think I've ever had a conversation with Nick Galina, just the two of us.

"So listen," he says, brushing his hair out of his eyes. "I'm going to leave him here for the night. But it's getting cold, so I brought a blanket and a pillow."

I nod.

"I feel funny leaving him here."

"I bet," I say.

"The pillow's overkill, right?"

"Maybe."

"He's not a terrible guy or anything. He's pretty nice when he's not wasted. He's a double agent. Dad by day, drunk by night."

"Has he done rehab?"

"Four times. Never works."

I tell him about my dad, in and out five times, and

always started drinking again. "We could call Gus. We can ask him." I stand up, feeling excited by having a reason to call him.

Nick shakes his head. "I know what Gus will say. He'll say leave him where he landed. He'll say no blanket, no pillow."

I nod, knowing that's exactly what Gus will say. I sit back down.

"Look, he's got some kind of funky crud." Nick walks over to his dad and lifts his pant leg. "See that crap on his leg?"

I walk over and even in the dark I can see it. "That is funky."

"I mean, I don't want it to get infected or anything."

"I've got Bactine at home. I can run home and get—"

"No, Rosie, that's okay. I mean, I should cover him, right? Cover that funky crud."

"Of course."

"But Gus would say leave him where he landed. Leave him as he is."

"The blanket, but not the pillow," I say, surprising myself. I say it like I know what I'm talking about. The only thing I know is what will make Nick feel better.

"Okay, then." He looks out at the water and then sits down on the dock again. "I was going to call you or that Sherry girl, the one with the nose ring. She seems smart too, but she also seems like kind of a snot. I knew you wouldn't be snotty."

"I'm not snotty!" I cry happily, sitting down next to him.

He slides his eyes over to me and laughs. I laugh too. He tucks his hair behind his pink ear. "Now, your sister," he says. "She seems a little snotty."

I think about this. "She can be, a little maybe. But she's mostly just herself, and once you get to know her, she's, you know, *real.*"

"I used to see her and Perry Brockner on the boardwalk sometimes. In the summer, I work the kiddie coaster on Pier One."

I nod. "So how do I seem smart?"

"Just nice and quiet. When I look across the room at you at the meetings I can see you're thinking about stuff, I can see your wheels turning. You're not one of these giddy goofy girls, like Maureen Willy." He imitates her high, shrieking laugh in homeroom. "I hate that."

"You think I'm serious?"

He nods. "I'm serious."

I imagine my brain firing off little sparks, the wheels and levers cranking in my head. Little streams of smoke come out my ears. "Isn't it nice to be easy, though?" I say, stretching out my legs and giving them a wiggle. "To laugh and have fun . . ."

Nick looks down into the sand. "Well, I laugh."

"I know," I say quickly.

It's quiet down here. The only sounds are the water licking the shore, the cattails rustling, and the soft snore of Nick's dad. Nick stands and shakes open the blue blanket. With one quick move he covers his snoring father from the neck down. "Okay," he says.

"Good," I say.

I walk my bike and we start up the street. Nick looks back at his sleeping, drunken dad and shakes his head. "I can hardly believe the dude. Pisses me off royally."

A little ways up the street Nick points. "Here's my place." The house is small, with a nice porch filled with bicycles and surfboards. All the windows are lit. In the yard, a rowboat lies upside down on the stones. A girl with a stubby ponytail drags the recycle bin to the street in her slippers. She's got Nick's long legs. "Are we leaving him there or what?"

"Leaving him."

"My sister," Nick says as the girl heads back to the house.

"Where's your mom?" I ask, and blush. Maybe that's none of my business.

"Divorced," he says.

"You want some hot chocolate?" I ask. "I could make some."

"I better not. Have a whole freakin' chapter to read in American history." Nick looks down at his shoes and his hair falls into his face. "But thanks for coming, Rosie."

I've just started to pedal home when I hear "Wait." Nick runs up behind me. "I'll come," he says as I slow down. "I'll pedal." Nick stuffs the pillow into the basket and I sit with my arms around his waist. I can feel his hip bones and all his muscles working, pumping the pedals. He's skinny but strong. We ride like that up to the ocean, to my place. While I put the bike in the shed Nick stands at the kitchen door, hugging his pillow.

Inside, I get the chocolate going, moving around the kitchen, opening cupboards and lining up the unsweetened cocoa, sugar, and vanilla. I used to make hot chocolate with plain old Nestlé Quik, but Angie's been teaching me how to make yummy stuff. She pokes her head into the kitchen, and I introduce Nick. Behind his back, Angie makes her fingers like scissors, like she wants to snip off his hair. I make eyes, like *Don't you dare say anything*. "Good night, guys," she says, flashing a smile. Then I hear her climbing the stairs.

I light the pumpkin Angie carved. It's got a big crazy smile and triangle eyes with eyelashes. After I pour the hot milk, I flip off the light and the kitchen is filled with the glow of pumpkin light. We can see the moon through the window. It's a strange feeling to be in my kitchen with this boy from my homeroom, a boy with secrets like mine. I hover over my steaming cup.

"What do you think of the meetings, Rosie?"

"It's less lonely . . . going there."

"It's liberating, I'll say that. Leave your freaking father in the sand! Who would have thought? But all the God stuff drives me batty." Nick takes a sip. "This rocks," he says, licking at the Cool Whip. "I just don't believe in

God." He slurps his drink and leaves a bit of chocolate mustache on his lip.

"Not even a little?" I ask.

"I really don't," Nick says, looking serious. "I'm just not a believer. But I'm not pissy about it either. I think of myself as a friendly atheist."

I don't think I could be an atheist. The world is an awfully big place, and it's too hard to imagine that someone or something didn't think it up. I can believe in God when I ride my bike on the boardwalk early in the morning and the sun shines over the ocean, making the water glitter. Or when I hang out my window and stare at the moon over the sea. I tell Nick all this. "I like to think *someone* is running the show."

Nick loops his hair behind his small ears. They turn a dark shade of pink. "I wish I could see some proof," he says.

"Once I thought an angel touched my arm." As soon as I say it my cheeks get hot.

"Really?"

"It's nothing." I shake my head.

"I want to hear this."

"No you don't."

"Come on, Rosie," he says, like I should trust him.

So I tell him, even though I've never told this to anyone. A couple of years ago my dad lost his job again, and went on a binge again, and curled up on the couch with his bottle of Old Crow. Skate didn't want to tell our grandparents because we would be shipped off, again, to the mainland to live with frightened old Mrs. Feeley and her smelly, yappy dogs. So we kept our mouths shut and ate baked potatoes every night because we had a big five-pound bag. Skate used babysitting money to buy cheese and salsa and hamburger. She lifted stuff too, like tampons and toothpaste, stuff we needed, but I skip this part. She didn't get caught. It was a terrible time, a cold winter, and we waited until our grandparents were due back from Florida a month later. We ate potatoes. Skate was bitchy. My best friend, Carrie, had moved far away—Illinois might as well have been the moon. It didn't seem like Dad would ever get off the couch. He lay under a quilt embroidered with stars, drinking and sleeping and gurgling to himself. One morning, I lay in bed, feeling like a stone. I said, *Help me.* I didn't think I could get out of bed. *Help me,* I said. I felt a hand on my shoulder. I show Nick the spot, putting my fingers on the very place where I remembered the touch. "Right here," I say. Nick looks at my arm and blinks. I knew I'd been touched by something. I knew I wasn't alone. I was no longer a stone, just a girl cold in bed. I was able to climb out of the covers.

I can see Nick's wheels turning. He looks up at the ceiling. "Is the house drafty?"

"Yes. But it didn't feel like air, you know. It felt like a *hand.*"

Nick nods. "I don't mean to be a jerk."

"It's okay." But I feel dumb, telling him all that. "Maybe I needed to feel it, so I made it up."

"Maybe," Nick says. "But the thing that gets me, if there's some creator, if someone's in charge, then why aren't they *in charge*? I mean, why are soldiers and civilians dying every day in Iraq, why are millions of people being raped and driven out of villages in Darfur, why are . . ." He stops and scratches his head. "If there's a creator, why create crap? Why?" He pushes his hair off his face and his ears are flaming pink.

"I just don't know," I say.

Nick stretches and looks pleased with himself. "I'm just saying, I'm just saying . . ."

"I guess if I didn't believe in anything at all I would feel like an ant. Or maybe I am an ant. Maybe we're all ants."

"I'm not an ant, but if you want to be one . . . ," Nick says, and smiles.

"You don't need to think of me as an ant, okay?" I smile too.

"I don't at all. You're definitely not antlike. Not with those braids, anyway. No such thing as a hip-hop ant." He smiles and ducks his head, and his hair falls over his face, covering him.

Why should it make me feel good that I am definitely not antlike? I touch my braids.

"What's it like?" Nick asks. "For your father to be in jail? If you don't mind me asking."

Skate told everyone the first night we went to the meeting that our father was locked up. Gus asked her how she felt about that and she said, "He ripped off Walgreens and landed his ass in jail. It wasn't his first offense. How do you think I feel?" Gus said he didn't know and asked her to tell us. But she just stared at him like he was a moron.

"You don't have to tell me," Nick says.

I shrug. "The good news about being locked up is he can't drink. Maybe this will be the time he finally, finally stops."

Nick nods. "Maybe mine needs to get thrown in jail too." We sit there drinking our hot chocolate and then Nick starts to laugh and I do too. I don't know why, but we do.

"Skate won't visit him. I think she hates him."

"Do you sometimes hate him?"

I feel myself blush. "Oh, I get mad and stuff, but no, I don't hate him."

"I hate my dad," Nick says. "Right now I'm hating him."

But you love him too, I want to say. In my mind, I see Nick whipping open the blue blanket and resting it on top of his snoring dad. Nick sighs deeply, as if he's read my mind. He clasps his hands behind his head, and his T-shirt is wet beneath the armpits. "What a crapload we have to deal with."

When Nick gets up to use the bathroom, I pull his

pillow toward me. It has a blue striped pillowcase. I rest my head on it. It's squishy and smells like laundry soap and something else, like the warm-skin smell in the crook of your elbow. I bury my nose in the pillow. When the toilet flushes, I quickly lift my head.

"Thanks for everything," Nick says, picking up the pillow and giving it a punch.

"You did the right thing."

"I'll see you in homeroom," he says, slipping out the door. He turns back. "Thanks, Rosie."

Then he's gone. I climb up to the third floor and open the window in the front junk room. I sit on an end table and watch Nick, the friendly atheist, walk down the street with a striped pillow under his arm.

Skate

"Listen, Skate, don't get mad," Perry says.

"Don't you dare!" I twist the phone cord in my hand. Right now he should be zooming down the parkway in his Hyundai, coming home to me. Instead he's walking across campus to the amphitheater, where he works part-time selling tickets in the box office.

"Look, someone called in sick this weekend, and I need the money."

"Tough, Perry. Tell them to find someone else." In the background I hear street noise, a car horn.

"What? I'm having trouble hearing you. Look, I promise we'll get together soon. I'll call you later." A car whizzes by and then the line is dead.

This is supposed to be our weekend. The whole weekend. From this very morning to sunset tomorrow night. "He bailed," I tell Julia as she loads sticky plates into the dishwasher.

"Oh, Skate," she says, looking up at me. She turns

on the dishwasher and the low rumble of water fills the room. "He's always complaining about money. . . . You okay?" She squeezes my shoulder and we both look out the window, where the sun glints on the lagoon. I nod, but I don't mean it. A family of ducks swims by—the mom, I guess, and a string of little ones behind. Perry and I were going to have the whole weekend.

I ride up to Lucky's, where Frank is sitting at the prize counter eating a donut and wearing a Yankees cap backward. I slide into a seat next to him. "Why the face?" he asks. I tell him, and he offers me a bite of chocolate donut. "Maybe Brockner's got a thing going up there."

"He doesn't have a *thing.*"

"The guy sounds pretty lame to me. What are you gonna do?"

"I'm going up there." Once I say it I know it's true. I'm going to head up to Rutgers.

Frank bounces a yellow SuperBall against the counter. "Not wise, LD. Lay low. Don't return his calls. Worry him a little."

I slump on the counter. "What *is* it with him? He thinks he can put us on hold or something. Every time I talk to him he's rushing off to class, or to his job or wherever. It's always about *him.* What about *us,* what about *me*?" I take the keys from behind the counter and turn on the fortune-teller machine. It lights up and the mannequin moves her stiff fingers over the ball before the card shoots out. *Follow your heart's desire,* it says. I slide it into my pocket before Frank asks to see it.

"You want my advice?"

"No offense, Frank, but no."

He leans in close and his stubbly cheek scrapes mine. "Stubborn girl."

"You don't know him the way I do," I say, snatching the SuperBall. I bounce it hard against the floor and it flies toward the ceiling.

"Don't go," Frank sings.

"I'm going." I catch the ball in a clean swipe.

I met Perry last year at the water fountain. He was a senior and I was a sophomore. It was October but the days were still long and hot with summer, and we all sat sweaty in the classrooms. There he was, this pretty boy— tall, with dark glossy hair and the darkest eyes. When I leaned over to get a drink, he held my hair for me. He didn't do it to be funny or to flirt. He did it to be nice. Then he started to say hi to me in the hallway, and sometimes between second and third periods he'd stand between the buildings and I'd have to pass by him, his black hair looking almost blue in the sunlight. When I thought about him and wondered what he was like, I felt something soft. I wasn't used to that soft feeling, like something you could sink into if you wanted to. I kept seeing him. He seemed to be everywhere that October.

After school one day I carried my board out to the

road and there he was, all at once, standing next to me. "You keep turning up, don't you?" I said, squinting into the sun.

He looked me right in the eyes. "I think I want to like you," he said.

And I felt that soft thing again, and I didn't like feeling it, so I told him I had to go and got on my board and rode away.

But I have to tell you how I felt. Relieved, yeah. But also flattened, like a plastic bag under a speeding car. I didn't expect to feel *that*. He was just a boy in the twelfth grade who didn't know a thing about me or my life or my loser dad. Yet I couldn't help feeling like I'd lost something. It didn't make sense.

The next day after school he tried again. Oh, how I liked him for trying again.

"Hey, Skate." He knew my name! "I'm Perry."

I *know*, I wanted to say, but I just smiled.

It's funny how boys sometimes get tongue-tied. He opened his mouth like he was going to say something else, but then he just stood there with his hands buried in his pockets. So I helped him out. I rolled backward on my board. "You still want to like me?"

He nodded and looked over my shoulder. "I definitely do."

And then his friends pulled up in an old rattling Honda. "Hey, dude, are you coming or are you yakking?" one of them asked. They hung out the window, checking me out and teasing.

"I'm yakking. Give me a minute," he told them. Then he said to me, "We're going to the soccer game. Otherwise I'd rather yak."

"We can yak some other time."

"There's a bonfire tomorrow on the beach in the Heights. I hope you'll come." And then he looked right at me.

"Okay."

He climbed in the junky Honda and they were off, their noise streaming out the car behind them. Boys, boys. Teasing, laughing, strutting boys. Cute boys. But in the backseat was a different one, one who didn't show off or goof it up. One who had a perfect face and was just, well, nice.

I take an afternoon train up to Rutgers. It's dark and cold when I get there, the wind whipping my hair around so that I have to tie it back with a rubber band. I ride my board over to Perry's dorm, and part of me doesn't even want to see him. As some kids come out, I slip inside and tap on Perry's door. Simon answers and blinks at me. He slowly brushes his hair out of his eyes, like a guy who spends too much dang time thinking about his hair.

"Hey, I'm looking for Perry."

Simon scrunches his face. "Isn't he working?"

"He was, earlier today," I say.

"So are you, like, going to wait?" he asks with his hand on the doorknob, clearly not wanting me to come in.

I nod, not wanting to park myself on the beanbag again.

"I'm going out," he says.

"Okay." I slide by him and sit on Perry's bed. Simon checks his hair in the mirror, fluffs it out, and looks at his shirt. He pulls it off and digs in his closet for a new one. He's got some hair on his chest, not like Perry. He finds a blue T-shirt decorated with a palm tree, then sniffs the other shirt and shoves it in his laundry bag. He looks at himself in the mirror and does that fluffy hair thing again. "Looking good," I can't resist saying. He slides his eyes over to me, giving me a wicked dirty look. I flop back on Perry's bed with my arms over my head.

"Make sure the door is locked if you leave," he says, grabbing his keys.

"Yup," I say.

He stares at me. "Perry's expecting you?"

"I'm his girlfriend," I say as nicely as I can. I cross my ankles, wanting him to beat it already.

Simon sticks his wallet into his pocket, puts on a jean jacket, and doesn't say goodbye, just kind of gives me a flat fish-mouth smile and leaves.

Then I wait. I read *The Member of the Wedding* for a while. In the minifridge there's a jar of grape jelly. I find a slice of bread and make myself a little sandwich. I leave the sticky jelly knife on Simon's desk. What's that girl's name who lives upstairs? Ellie, I think. I could visit her—she seemed nice—but I don't know. There's a knock on the door and a tall guy with feathery hair stands there. "You're not Simon," he says.

"Thank God for that."

"Ouch." He leans in the doorway and tilts his head, checking me out. He's cute in a slouchy, cocky way. Freckles are sprinkled across his nose and cheeks.

"I'm Olivia," I say. "Perry's girlfriend."

"Hey, Olivia, I'm Johnny. So where's Perry?"

"He'll be here."

"And I guess Simon left. . . ."

I flick my wrist. "Off into the night." His eyes graze over my face. I always like this part—watching a boy like what he sees. I let him look. "Can I borrow your cell for a minute?" I ask.

"I guess," he says.

He walks into the room and hands it to me and sits on the edge of Perry's desk. "Dude," I say. "How about a little privacy, please?"

"Okay then." He backs out of the room, looking at me the whole time.

I close the door and sit on the floor. Perry's line rings once and goes right to voice mail. Where is he! I hang up and call again. Same thing the second time, and when I hear the tone I can't bring myself to say anything. I dial Rosie.

"Where are you?" she says.

"Out. Don't ask."

"I can't talk long. I'm meeting Nick. We're going for a walk."

"Nick who?"

"From the meetings. You know, he's the one—"

"Are you hanging out with those people now?"

" 'Those people'? Aren't *we* 'those people'? Nick's nice. You'd like him. Are you at Rutgers?"

"Yeah."

"Oh, Skate, I should go. Nick will be—"

"Let him wait a minute."

"Are you okay?" Rosie asks.

"Well, yeah," I say, looking around the empty room. I hear the tick of Perry's alarm clock and the hum of the refrigerator. "Don't you want to talk for a minute?"

"Would you stop coming home so late? I hardly ever see you. Sometimes you're here, sometimes not. I never know where you are."

"Rosie, relax already."

"Did you write Dad yet?"

"For your information, I did, nosey."

"You did! That's good, Skate. You mailed it?"

"I will."

"I can mail—"

"Ai-yi-yi, Rosie. What a naggola you are. *I'll* mail it."

"Does Perry know you're there?"

"Yeah," I lie. "We're hooking up in a little while."

"I really have to go now, Skate. Promise me I'll see you tomorrow."

I tell her she will.

I find Johnny sitting on the beanbag playing solitaire. "Hey," I say. "Do you want to play cards?"

"How about poker?"

I tilt my head and look at him. "I should tell you I'm *good*." We decide to make it interesting by playing for nickels and dimes. Johnny lives in the dorm next door, and when he returns with a cup full of change we head back to Perry's room and sit on the floor. The Old Crow taught Rosie and me how to play years ago. While Johnny shuffles, I dump open my wallet and pick out nickels and dimes, and then I dig through Perry's drawers and come up with another dollar in change.

Well, I'm on a roll. A half hour later, I've won game after game, and most of Johnny's stash.

"You're pretty lucky."

"Yup," I say, sweeping my winnings into a pile.

He turns his mug upside down and he's nearly cleaned out. "I guess I quit." He lies on the floor and looks up at me.

"You can't quit," I say, looking at the clock and then at the door. "Come on."

"You wanna play strip poker?" he asks with a smile.

Ha! "Be careful what you wish for. I'll have you down to your undies in no time." Little does he know I have on, like, three layers of shirts. Plus I'm winning. What fun!

But then my luck turns, and he wins hand after hand. Between us is a pile of my stuff: socks, sneakers, toe ring, sweatshirt, button-down shirt, belt, earrings. I'm down to my jeans and T-shirt, and honestly, I like the idea of Perry walking in on this little scene. Serves him right. Except he doesn't show, and I lose another hand. Johnny smiles real slow. "Sorry, my friend," he says. I have on only five things—my T-shirt, jeans, bra, underwear, and necklace. I'm not taking off my necklace—Perry gave it to me for Christmas—it's a tiny silver heart and I wear it always. So what the hell, I'll give him a little thrill. I reach under my tee and unhook my bra. It's my one nice bra—purple, lacy, and slippery. I slide the strap off one arm, then the other, and throw it on the pile. "This is where I quit."

"You can't quit on me now," he says.

"I can and I am."

He picks up my bra and touches it gently. "Give me that," I say, grabbing it.

"Sorry," he says, letting it go. "It's sexy."

"Perry thinks so," I say, holding his gaze 'cause I don't want his eyes roaming over my boobs even if I am wearing a T-shirt.

"Where's your boyfriend anyway? Weird you're here and he isn't."

"What's that supposed to mean?"

"Nothing," he says, leaning back on his elbows and staring at me.

"Well . . ." I yawn. "I'm done here." I gather my pile of stuff and start putting myself back together, except for the bra, of course, which I can't put back on without taking off my shirt.

"Want a beer?"

"No thanks."

Johnny reaches for my bra, running his finger over it. I snatch it away and toss it on Perry's bed. "I really don't get the feeling Perry's coming back," he says, watching me. "We can hang out in my room."

"I called him a little while ago," I lie. "He's just running late."

I slip on the button-down shirt and belt my jeans. Johnny watches me.

"Are you in high school?"

"Maybe, maybe not," I hear myself say. God, I sound stupid! Where is Perry? *Where!*

He stands and stretches and checks me out, and then leans in close. "You know, your boyfriend hangs out with a lot of people. . . ."

"So? So do I."

"Does he actually know you're here?" And I feel my

face grow warm, knowing that Johnny knows Perry doesn't know I'm here in his room. "Don't be stupid, Olivia," he whispers. He reaches out and touches my hair where it brushes my waist. "You're something, you know that?"

"You think you're the first boy to tell me that?" I move away and sit on Perry's bed and put on my socks and sneakers.

"So you're stuck-up?" He sits on the floor and looks up at me. "Is that what you're saying?"

"I think you should go."

"Your boyfriend's not waiting for *you,* now, is he? Come to my room. We can have a beer and talk. You'll tell him you waited long enough."

"Just go," I say. But I can't seem to get mad, and my voice is soft.

"I'll go," he says, but he stays where he is and stretches out on the floor. He lifts up the bottom of his shirt and drums his fingers on his stomach. "Oh-livia," he says, drawing it out.

"What do you mean Perry hangs out with lots of people?"

"Just what I said."

"Who?"

"It must be hard for you with him here. . . ."

"Do you mean Gina?"

"I know Gina," he says, and smiles. "Gi-nah!"

"I think it's time for you to bounce." I open the door.

"Jealous?"

I shake my head, remembering her dark gleaming hair.

"You're hot too, Olivia," he whispers, "but you're not here."

"Go."

"Gone." He gets up and smiles and backs out the door. "I'm next door. One-oh-one, if you change your mind. I have beer and weed."

I shut the door and lock it. Then I sit at Perry's desk and open the drawers, one by one, not even knowing what I'm looking for. I paw through papers, notebooks, pens, a razor, a comb, a picture of me doing a cartwheel on the dunes, a calculator, a stick of cinnamon gum. Scribbles and phone numbers. Math equations, a green marble, a beer cap. Lots of stuff. Nothing.

It's late when I crawl under his covers.

"Get up." He's shaking me hard.

"Perry," I say, jumping up.

"He's not here, stupid. Get up and get out." Simon flips on the light, and he's standing there with a girl and they're holding bottles of beer. She gives me one of Simon's fish smiles. Simon leans in close and yanks me up. "I have the room tonight. You have to get out."

"Okay. Stop grabbing me." I shove my purple bra under Perry's pillow and grab my stuff and leave.

"Christ," Simon says, shutting the door. "Can you believe her?"

It's 3:30 in the morning. I sit on the beanbag, rubbing my eyes, wondering what to do. All of a sudden, I know in my heart that Perry must have gone home to Little Mermaid to see me, and if I hadn't come up we would be together now.

I hurry to the train station, but it's closed. The first train of the day isn't until 5:25. The streets are brightly cold, and college kids are gathered here and there under the streetlights. I wander until I find a diner crowded with students having breakfast or dinner, eggs and toast or spaghetti or burgers. I sit at the counter and order a hot chocolate and mashed potatoes and gravy, and the waitress isn't exactly happy when I pay with all Johnny's nickels and dimes. There's lots of happy noise around me—plates clanking, talking, laughing. At one table a guy and girl are making out, at another a group of guys are leaning in close while one whispers something. In a booth, a girl braids another girl's hair. Across from them another girl yawns daintily and then smiles at the room. As I sit there chewing and watching and listening, I think maybe Perry isn't in Little Mermaid after all, that he's somewhere in this night.

Back home, I ride my board past Julia's house. No Hyundai. No Perry. I ride up to the beach and sit on the dunes. The morning sun is fierce, so bright on the waves I have to squint. This—all this—is my home. This is Perry's home too. Rutgers is a pit stop, but it's not home. I know he knows this. I walk the beach toward my house and climb the stairs to my room.

Rosie

On Halloween everybody ditches the meeting, including Skate, who wouldn't budge an inch. "I have plans," she said.

"What kind of plans?" I demanded.

"Plans not to go," she said, giving me a wicked smile. "Maybe I'll hang out with Frank." And she zipped herself into her sweatshirt and took off down the street on her skateboard. Something's up with her and Perry. He keeps calling and she keeps pretending not to be home—that is, when she *is* at home. Most of the time I don't know where the heck she is.

So it's just me, Gus, Nick, and a tray of Gus's orange-iced cupcakes decorated with candy corn. Gus wears a beanie with googly eyes attached to two springy antennas, which gives me a reason to smile at him—him sitting there all goofy and cute. He definitely knows how to have fun. Skate is just wrong.

Nick gives us an update on his dad. Most nights,

lately, he manages to get himself to bed; sometimes he lands on the sofa. He hardly ever sleeps on the sand anymore. But this morning Nick found him on the kitchen floor.

"So what did you do?" Gus asks.

"I left him where he landed, like you always say. I stepped over him and made myself a slice of toast."

"There you go!" Gus says. Nick shrugs.

Gus looks at me, and I feel my face grow warm. "You're always the quiet one, Rosie. What's up with you?"

"I'm okay." He waits, smiling at me. "I just wish my sister was here."

"Maybe she'll turn up again. Give her time."

I shake my head. "She won't deal with our dad. She'll never forgive him."

"Maybe she's not ready to," Nick says.

"She'll never be ready. . . ."

"Do you forgive him?" Gus asks.

"This is going to sound weird," I say, smoothing out my skirt with my palms. "But jail is probably the best thing that could have happened. He's stuck there, he can't drink. This time he's bound to get his act together. Don't you think so?"

"Could be," Gus says. "But you don't need to fix everything, Rosie. Leave Skate to Skate, and your dad to himself."

"I *can't*."

"You can *try*," he says, leaning toward me.

"But I don't think I can. . . ."

"Take a baby step. Little eensy step." Gus holds up two fingers an inch apart. "Next week don't beg your sister to come. Just say bye and walk out the door."

"Then she won't come!"

"She doesn't come when you try!"

"I know!" Then I laugh and think about that. "That's so totally true." I pluck up a cupcake, swish my finger through the icing, and lick it clean.

Nick gives me a sly look and leans back in his chair, clasping his hands behind his head. "Gus, dude, do you ever get tired of listening to us? All our crap?"

"It's good to figure out the crap."

Nick frowns and hooks his hair behind his ears. "Do we ever really figure out the crap?"

I shrug and unpeel my cupcake. Gus tilts his head from side to side, jiggling his goofy antenna. "Maybe, maybe not," he says.

"Okay, screw it," I say. "Next week I'll just say bye and walk out the door." They both look at me, surprised.

Afterward, Gus walks outside with us and gets in his beat-up car. I wonder if he has plans, it being Halloween and all. Nick and I get on our bikes. "Want to come over and help me hand out candy?" I ask.

"I got a better idea. There's a party in the Heights. You game?"

A party! What a terrifying prospect—a party! "Yes," I blurt out before I have time to talk myself out of it. Above us is a perfect Halloween moon, full and bright in the sky. "But we don't have costumes."

"We have a bunch of stuff in the attic. I can probably dig you up a pointy hat or something."

"Hey, you're not trying to tell me something, are you?"

"You're totally nice, Rosie," Nick says, ducking his head to hide a smile. "Not the least bit witchy."

So we ride our bikes over to Nick's house and go in the side door, where his sister, Amy, is making Jiffy Pop at the stove. I call Angie and she says, "A party, huh? That'll be fun, Ro." But I can tell she's going to miss me, that I won't be there with her to hand out Tootsie Pops and Milky Ways.

Nick cocks his head toward the living room, where his dad is sprawled on the couch, watching TV. "I'll make it quick," he tells me, scooting up the stairs.

Amy burns her fingers peeling open the hot foil and yelps. "Yow!" she cries. "Here. Have some." I finger some out of the hot pieces and place them sizzling on my tongue.

Their dad heaves himself off the couch. "Come up," Amy whispers in my ear. But before I know it she's scurried up the stairs with the Jiffy Pop while their dad moves slowly toward me. His rubs his bright and glassy face with one of his hands. "A girl in the kitchen," he booms.

I lift my hand to say hi. He turns on the faucet and watches the water fall. Then he wets his fingers and dries them slowly on a paper towel. I spot a bottle half-hidden behind the microwave. That's what he wants. But he won't pour any in front of me. This I know.

"And what's your name?"

"Angie," I say, not looking at him.

"How do you do, Angie girl? Which kid are you here for?"

"Nick."

"Good kid, that Nicky. But do me a favor," he says, leaning toward me and showing all his teeth in a crazy smile. "Tell him to get a haircut already. Boys looking like girls. Chop it the hell off!"

I give him a tiny smile.

"A girl in the kitchen," he singsongs. He takes a beer out of the fridge, places it on the counter, and stares at the bottle as if he's going to ask it a question. Then he seems to forget about it and makes his way back to the living room, where he bumps an end table, wobbling the lamp and making the light flicker. He flops down on the couch with a groan.

Nick flies down the steps and hands me a witch's hat with a little plastic bat dangling from the pointy tip, and a long black cape. For himself he has an executioner's mask, sword, and cape. He draws on my cheek with a black eye pencil. He leans close to me, and his light brown eyes are the color of candy caramels.

"What are you drawing?" He drags me over to the chrome of the refrigerator, where I see a little spider on my cheek. "Perfect!" I say, suddenly in a party mood.

"Come on," Nick says, whizzing out the door. I swipe the beer from the counter and hide it in the folds of my cape. We ride over to the beach in the Heights and leave our bikes on the sand. A lit house thumps with music. I pull out the bottle, twist off the cap, and hand it to Nick.

"You didn't!" he says.

"I did," I say gleefully.

"Rosie, you little thief," Nick says, giving me a playful shove.

"Screw it."

"Listen to you and your 'screw its'! What's up with you?" I give him a happy shrug. Nick takes a long sip and hands me the beer. I take a long sip too. We pass it back and forth until it's gone, and I'm a little woozy as I put on my hat and cape.

Inside, music pulses through the rooms. Nick gets us each a foamy cup of beer, and we wander through the packed rooms, sipping our drinks. There's a slutty nun, a doctor called Dr. Perv, a hairy gorilla, some punk surfers, assorted ghouls, a tomato smoking a joint. Leaning against a windowsill are two guys from our homeroom—one dressed as a hamburger, the other a hot dog. On the front porch we sit on the staircase, drinking and watching everybody.

"Let's dance," I say, crushing my empty cup.

"Nuh-uh. I don't dance."

"Come on. It'll be fun." Nick groans as I pull on his arm.

We weave our way back inside, where it's dark now except for candles burning in the windows. There's hardly a space as we squeeze in. Oh, it feels good to dance! As I twirl, the little bat flies around my head. I smile at Nick and he rolls his eyes, but he bends his knees and bops along to the Stones. A girl from my biology class dressed as a harem girl waves to me and I wave back. Across the room, a girl and guy from the meetings smile at us.

I shake my hips from side to side and Nick laughs. All together we sing:

"I said I know it's only rock 'n' roll but I like it, like it, yes, I do!"

Oh, how good it feels to dance! I look into the shimmering candlelight, feeling filled up with the thumping music that beats like a heart. A guy dressed as a shark stabs me with his fin. "Sorry," he says, twirling me in a circle, his face happy and sweaty.

"No problem," I shout above the music. We go on pulsing and twisting, the music ricocheting around us.

Nick's face is shiny with sweat. "I'm out," he says. He sits on the floor with his back against a wall.

"Let's have more beer," I say, leaning down to him.

"I'm cutting you off, dudette," he says.

I guess I am pretty tipsy, so I dance and dance, all giddy, until my head's so sweaty that my hat won't stay on. I see Nick staring up at me from the floor. He tilts his head and gives me the nicest smile and reaches out to touch my whirling cape.

Finally, out of breath, I join Nick on the floor. "Let's get some air," he says. We squeeze through the crowd and run out to the dunes, where the chill is like a slap in the face. But it feels *good*. Nick spreads out his cape and we lie back on it on the sand.

"I wish I had a cigarette," he says.

"You smoke?"

"Only sometimes."

"Oh, Nick. That's gross."

"Yeah, I know."

I stare at the stars and cover a handful with my out-stretched arm. "School tomorrow," I say.

"Rosie," Nick whispers. "Have you ever had sex?"

"What?" I say.

"I'm just asking."

"I can't believe you asked me that."

"Don't get bent out of shape," he says. "I'm just cu-rious, that's all."

"Have you?"

He shakes his head. "No. But I wouldn't mind."

Me, I would just like to be kissed, but I don't say that. What I think about is a boy looking into my eyes and me looking into his. I imagine the moment soft and romantic, a slow-motion moment, where at the last second I lower my eyes and he kisses me softly on the lips, again and again, then me raising my eyes and kissing him back.

"Back there," Nick says, gesturing with his thumb, "who do you think is doing it? What about the hamburger and hot dog?"

"With each other or with girls?"

"Hey, maybe they *are* gay . . . ," Nick says, scratching his chin.

We decide John and Alan, the hamburger and hot dog, are probably not doing it with girls or each other. The slutty nun, the diapered baby, and the gorilla probably aren't either. The punk surfers, the tomato, Cleopatra, and the sumo wrestler—probably. But, my God, how is anyone supposed to really know something so private about someone else? "Well, not me," I say.

"Not me either."

"You already said that." I slide my eyes over at him and we laugh.

"You were a little lush tonight," Nick says.

"Oh, I was not."

"Come on, you were sucking those beers down."

"Don't." I slap him. "That's not funny."

"Relax."

"I hate to be told to relax."

"Touchy," he says, tickling me. I giggle and push his hand away. "Rosie, you're kind of pretty, you know that?"

I feel myself smile, and look down at my hands. It's then that I catch a glimpse of my watch. Midnight. Already. "Nick, I gotta go." I hop up and brush off the sand.

Nick pokes me. "When someone tells you you're pretty you're supposed to say thank you."

"But you only said 'kind of.'" I burst out laughing and clap my hand over my mouth. "I can't believe I said that."

Nick laughs and shakes his head. "What is *with* you tonight?"

"Full moon? I just don't know," I say, feeling happy. All I know is I want to dance, and I do a little twirl across the sand.

Nick picks up my bike and hands it to me. "Not 'kind of.' Just pretty." And even in the dark I see him blush. I meet his eyes, remembering the way he looked sitting against the wall, smiling up at me, his hand reaching out to touch my swirling cape.

"Thanks," I whisper, suddenly feeling shy. Then he leans across my bike and kisses me fast on the lips. He whisks his own bike out to the street, jumps on it, and pedals away.

Skate

Frank's between girlfriends, so here I am on his funky couch. I rotate—Frank's, my place, and sometimes even Julia's. I haven't completely cleared out of Julia's 'cause I miss her—miss talking to her and miss her macaroni and cheese with the crunchy top. But the weirder things get with Perry the less I want to be there. Plus I don't want to have to lie to her again. Angie thinks when I'm not at home I'm at Julia's. I let her think that. I don't like bouncing all around, but what can I do?

Sometimes I just want to stay home, in my very own room, but Rosie can be such a naggola, bugging me about this and that. Frank is easy. And his place isn't too bad. His couch is a big comfy lump where I bet he's made out with a million girls. He's made girls cry. I've seen some of them with their wet faces and puffy eyes and heard them yell at Frank. When that happens he seems to shrink down a size. He can't get away from those weepy girls fast enough. What a heartbreaker, that Frank.

The first night Frank covered the couch with sheets and gave me a soft blue blanket. He told me not to touch his beer, that he wasn't going to have any under-age drinking in his abode. Like I want one of his beers. "Relax," I told him.

Tonight Frank is in sweats and a dirty T-shirt with a toothbrush sticking out of his mouth. "So you get to see your boy tomorrow," he says with a foamy mouth.

"Yep." I sigh.

Frank waves the toothbrush at me, saying, "I bet he's going to love you staying here." He spits in the kitchen sink.

"He doesn't need to know, Frank." I slip under the soft blue blanket.

Frank takes hold of my foot under the covers and gives it a squeeze. "Good night, LD."

"Good night."

Frank pads into his bedroom, and I hear him plunk his toothbrush on the night table. The mattress squeaks as he climbs into bed.

Here's what happened: Perry found out from Simon I was there waiting for him. All week Perry's called and left messages with Julia, Rosie, and Angie, and he even called the arcade and spoke to Frank. But I didn't call him back. I let him call and call before finally I talked to him.

"I'm coming home Saturday morning, and I need to see you," he told me.

"Fine."

He kept saying, "Jesus, Skate, why didn't you call me? I didn't know you came up." *Because I thought you'd show up, Perry. I was in your room, where supposedly you live.* What I said, though, was "We'll talk when I see you." Then I hung up.

"Frank, you sleeping?"

"Yep," he yells back.

"Frank, you go through an awful lot of girls, you know that?"

"Go to sleep."

"I just want to know why."

"There are so many good ones I can't decide."

"Gimme a break."

"I like girls. Why shouldn't I?"

"Do you sleep with all of them?"

"Mind your business, LD." And I hear him yawn, a slow, lazy yawn.

"Come on, Frank."

"Well, I ain't talking."

Before Perry I slept with one other boy. He was a benny and I usually don't like bennies. A benny is a person who comes to the shore only in the summer and takes all the benefits. They drive big-ass SUVs and cause traffic jams, leave their sandwich wrappers on the sand, travel in packs with screaming fat-ass kids. The point is there are a lot of them; they clutter up the place and don't live here year-round. Frank, though, loves bennies. Where would we be without the bennies, he loves to say. They fatten up the local economy. *Cha-ching.* Anyway, I met a benny two summers ago. A cute benny with very blond hair and a sunburned nose. His grandparents rented a big old beauty of a house on the bay. We hung out and went surfing. We went to the little movie theater and slurped Italian ice and fooled around in the back row. And it was with the benny—I really should call him by his name—it was with Chris that I got naked all the way.

One night I thought we were both ready, so I took him by the hand and led him up the back staircase of my house to my room. We heard a crash below and Chris wanted to see what happened, but I told him, "It's all right, it's just my dad. He's a drunk." Before Perry, I'd never told anyone that, but since Chris was a benny I really didn't care.

"Oh, the poor toaster oven!" we heard the Old Crow wail. Chris shrugged and I did too, and we climbed to the third floor, where we slipped between my rumpled sheets. It was a cool August night and I opened the window wide so the curtains fluttered above us. We could hear the waves hitting the shore.

"Have you done this before?" I whispered as he slid off my jeans.

"Not really."

"I think the answer is yes or no."

He buried his face in my neck and whispered, "I tried once but had, you know, operating trouble. The girl was bitchy about it too."

"I won't be bitchy—I mean, if you have trouble."

"That's good," he said, looking at me shyly, his nose all pink and peeling. And we did it. It hurt and everything but it was still nice. He touched me like he was running his hands over something expensive. And I liked feeling him sprawled out against me, all that skin. We did it twice more before Labor Day and then he left. He called once, but without surfing and the little movie theater and getting naked we didn't really have much to say. That fall I met Perry by the water fountain. When summer rolled around again, I saw Chris once on the beach with another girl. I was with Perry. We waved to each other, but in my mind he was back to being a benny. I had Perry, the real thing in every which way. I didn't love Chris—I know that now, even though at the time I wondered because I liked him a lot—but I didn't.

I creep off the couch and stand in Frank's doorway. I hear him breathing and it sounds nice, all even and sleepy. I wish I could crawl in bed with him, just to sleep, just to feel a body next to me. So I lie down next to him but don't get under the covers, 'cause obviously that wouldn't be cool. I listen to the rise and fall of his breath. Not a care in the world, that Frank.

❊

I get there late. When I walk in, Perry's already forking up eggs. "Hello, stranger," I say to him as Julia hands me a glass of OJ.

"Come over here, you," Perry says with his mouth full.

"When I'm ready."

"Then I'll come over there."

He starts to get up out of his seat, but I say, "Sit. Eat." I give Julia a hug, and she shakes her head at the two of us.

She's made a feast—eggs and muffins and bacon and fried potatoes with tomatoes. I slip into a chair across from Perry, and he comes around the table and pecks me on the head. "Where have you been? I call here, your house, you're never anywhere."

"Oh, that's a good one," I say, but I can't help smiling a little—it's so *good* to see Perry. It is!

"Okay, you two—eat first, fight later," Julia says. She's eating yogurt with fresh strawberries but keeps reaching for the crunchy potatoes. Outside a horn beeps, and Julia looks at her watch and gasps. "That's Hal." She stuffs a potato in her mouth, grabs her coat, and runs with her yogurt container to the front door. "You guys will clean up?"

"Sure, Mom," Perry says.

Julia opens the door and waves. "Listen," she says, turning back to us. She looks like she's about to say something, but she just stands there sizing us up. "It's good to have you both here." And then she whisks herself out the door.

"Oh, Skate!" Perry gushes when she's gone.

"Not yet." Perry stares at me unhappily across the table as I load my plate. "Eat!" I tell him.

"So bossy, you are," he says, picking up his fork. When we're done he comes over and squeezes into my chair and kisses me for real, smelling like bacon and shampoo. His hair is still damp. "So . . . ," he says.

"Let's clean up first."

Perry rolls his eyes deliciously slow, but he rises from the table and gets the sink full of soapy water while I scrape plates. Then I sit at the counter and watch him wash dishes. He's slow and careful and lets the water drip off before he stacks them on the drainboard. His hair has gotten longer and he seems a little bit taller too, and he has on a faded blue T-shirt I don't recognize. What I want to do is go up behind him and slide my arms around him. I want to take him by the hand and go into his bedroom and get naked. But for some reason I can't. When Perry finishes the frying pan he turns around and faces me, and we stare at each other for a long time. Finally, he leads me to the couch, but everything I want to say is jumbled inside me, and I sit there like a dummy.

"I can't talk here," I say. "Let's go to the beach." I get on my board and ride, don't even wait for him to get his bike out of the shed. I take off my sneakers and run across the sand and stick my feet in the shivery cold November water. It's so cold it bites, and the wind whips my hair all over the place. When I turn, Perry is jogging toward me. He drops his sneakers in the sand and joins me. "Yow!" he says when a wave splashes over him. He scurries out of the water, tugging me along.

"How come you never showed that night?" I say.

"I didn't know you were in my room," he yells.

"I waited and waited and you never came. Simon threw me out at like three-thirty in the morning."

"Skate," Perry says, grabbing my arm, but I yank away. "Simon had the room last Saturday night. I was in the library, then I met up with some friends for strombolis, then I went to a party and later crashed on a friend's carpet. I had no idea you were in my dorm. Why the freak didn't you call?"

"Why? Is that what you want to know? Why?"

"Yeah. Why?"

"I did." I fly around and face him. "But I got your voice mail. I always get your voice mail. Sometimes you call back but mostly you don't." He lowers his eyes and I give him a shove. "You jerk. You're forgetting about me."

"No." He tries to grab me, and we land in the sand with me on his lap. "Listen," he says, but he doesn't say anything else.

"So talk," I say.

"I'm freaked, Skate. Nearly all the time." And then he tells me how it is. Always, always, he has too much to do and not enough time. Not all his grades are good. He wants to have friends and go out and be part of everything. Then there's his job, which eats up hours. And even so, he never has enough money. And he can't keep asking Julia for cash, he says, not with all the money she's shelling out for his dorm, meal plan, and tuition. So he has to work at least fifteen hours a week.

"It doesn't sound like there's room for me."

"There *has* to be room for you." His eyes fill with tears.

"Do you still love me, Perry?"

"I do. I love you, Skate."

We sit there for a while, just like that. He slides his hand under my T-shirt. His fingers are cold on my stomach but after a while they warm up.

The day turns out sort of weird, sort of happy. We walk the boardwalk, sneak into the amusement area, which is closed for the season, climb a ladder to the sky ride and sit in one of the cars with our legs dangling over the beach. We talk about all kinds of stuff—my classes, his teachers, where to get the best slice, the Old Crow, whether Julia will marry Hal, this kid we know who lost his brother in Iraq, how much we miss touching each other. When the sun pokes through the clouds, we head home to put on our wet suits and surf, but the waves are kind of dinky, so mostly we sit on our boards with the water lapping at us. Perry lets his board bump mine, and when he reaches out his hand I take it. In the late afternoon we both do homework at my kitchen table—Rosie and Angie are off visiting the Old Crow. In the middle of an equation, Perry looks up and offers to come home next weekend to go with me to the jail. "Don't promise anything you can't deliver," I say.

Perry looks genuinely wounded, and his neck even gets splotchy pink. "What must you think of me," he says. We have a stare-down until Perry says, "Okay, let me see how my week goes." I nod and shrug. When Rosie and Angie get home, the four of us make a big gooey tray of lasagna and sit around the kitchen eating. It's a good time, and Ro doesn't hassle me even once.

Later, back at Perry's house, we lie naked in his bed. We're not supposed to share a room—me and Perry— but sometimes Julia pretends like she doesn't notice. She's out with Hal anyway. I have my hand on Perry's chest and feel his heart beating fast and warm.

"I'm sorry for being such a lousy boyfriend."

"Honestly, dude, you've been pretty lousy lately."

"But in my defense," he says, and he sits up.

"Here we go," I say, 'cause I'm worn out from this day.

"Look, in my defense, you call me about five times a day. You're always leaving messages, really long messages."

"Look," I say, sitting up. "I'm just talking. You're my best friend. Can't you listen?"

He sighs. "Okay, I'm being a jerk." And he flops back on the pillow.

I give him a kick under the covers.

He hangs over the bed and fishes around in his duffel bag. He tosses me my nice purple bra. "Found this under my pillow. Are you the good fairy?" I run my fingers over the satin. "What were you doing?" he asks in a funny voice.

"I was sleeping in your bed. What do you think I was doing?" Remembering Johnny's fingers touching the bra, I let it drop to the floor.

We lie there for a long time, and I'm nearly asleep when something comes to me and snaps me wide awake. "Perry," I say, giving him a shake.

"What?" he says, all sleepy, curling away from me.

"Wake up."

He groans.

"You said Simon had the room that night. That must mean *you* have it some nights. But you never once invited me up."

He groans again. "Skate, you're still in high school. What am I supposed to do? You're living with my *mom*. She's not going to let—"

I'm about to tell him I don't really live with Julia anymore, but something holds me back. "So what do *you* do when you have the room?"

"I have wild orgies with naked girls."

"Answer me."

He groans again. "Look, I clear out some Saturday nights so Simon and his girl-of-the-week can have the room. Simon helps me with calculus. He's a math whiz. It's our deal." I think about this. "Go to sleep," Perry says. But we lie there, not sleeping. "That night," he says after a while, "were you talking to that creep Johnny?"

"Kind of. He was the *only* one around, Perry."

"He's a real creep."

"Simon's a real creep too."

"He's good in math."

"Well, that math whiz threw me out in the middle of the night."

Perry slaps his pillow, his voice angry. "If you'd called me—if I knew you were in my dorm that never would have happened."

"If you answered your damn phone that never would have happened."

"Can we just sleep?"

"Be my guest," I say. But I feel him wide awake next to me. It's a relief when I hear Julia's car door. I throw on underwear and a T-shirt and take my pillow to the spare room, where I curl up on the couch alone.

Rosie

"Boys are like that," Angie says, working her gum. We're sitting in the ugly gray visiting room at one of the long tables, and I'm fingering my stack of quarters. "Just play it cool and he'll come back around."

"I guess," I say. "It's weird, right?"

Ever since that little kiss on the beach, Nick's been acting different. He's still nice and all—yesterday after lunch we leaned against the lockers, sharing a bag of potato chips—but we haven't exactly been hanging out. At three o'clock he's either nowhere to be found or he has his nose in a book on the bus ride to the island. "See you," he says, jumping out when we reach his stop.

"Maybe he regrets kissing me."

"I seriously doubt it," Angie says, grinning. "Boys have this weird thing called the 'freak factor.' His freak factor is on high. Just pretend that all is well and, guess what, it probably will be. He needs some space, so let him have it."

"It was just the littlest kiss. . . ."

"Freak factor."

"Oh, boy," I say, shaking my head. We both laugh. I have to confess I don't get it.

And while we're talking about Nick, the room has filled up with men in their orange jumpsuits, but my dad isn't here. Angie and I look at each other and then at the door. A few more minutes pass, and he still isn't here. I look at Angie.

"Let's find out," she says.

The guard pulls out an enormous set of keys to open a set of double doors. He takes us into a small cramped room with a metal table and some chairs. Up high is a barred window. "Wait here," he says.

Something bad has happened. I know it. But I can't bear to say those words aloud. I sit and rub my sweaty palms on my knees and say a tiny prayer: *Please, no.* Soon the warden comes in, a bulky man with a bushy mustache that hangs over his upper lip. He sits down heavily. The chair creaks, and he folds his hands. "Folks, some bad news." I stare at his fleshy neck. "Mr. Meyers's visitation rights have been revoked." My dad, he tells us, broke into the pharmacy late last night and downed bottles of cough syrup. For the alcohol. To get intoxicated.

"No," I say, blinking.

The warden eyes me, not unkindly, but he keeps talking. He tells us my dad is in solitary confinement awaiting disciplinary action.

"What do you think will happen to him?" Angie asks.

"Could be a number of things." He leans back and fingers his mustache. "It's possible he could have his sentence extended."

"No," I say again, whipping my head from Angie to the warden. *Cough syrup?* I picture the grape formula we have in the medicine cabinet. I imagine drinking a bottle, then another, then another. Unbelievable.

And before I know it, the enormous keys reappear and we're being led out another door. I can't seem to get myself to walk, and Angie gives me a tug.

"I have to see him," I say, turning back to the warden.

"I can't do that," he says. "I'm sorry," he adds.

"Doesn't he know I'm counting down the days?" I shout to Angie. "Why?"

"Rosie, come on," Angie whispers.

"I have to see him," I wail. And I can't stop. Angie has to peel my fingers off the door. "I have to!" I shout. "I really have to." And next thing I know, two guards grab me, one on either side, and pull me toward the exit. It's all in slow motion, and I'm crying by the time we reach the sunny parking lot.

Angie tries to hold me but I whirl around, shouting, "It's a mistake, a mistake. How could he?"

Finally, I let her hug me. "I know, Rosie. I know. It's totally screwed," she whispers.

❄

Angie wants to do something nice, maybe cook up a big meal or go to a movie, but I have to see Skate. When we get back to Little Mermaid, I ride my bike over to Julia's, but the house is dark. Then I ride over to the arcade, which is pretty empty this time of year. Frank is fixing a Skee-Ball alley and Skate is sprawled out in the alley next to him, like she's sunbathing. As soon as I see her I burst into tears.

"What?" Skate says, sitting up and grabbing my wrist.

I can't talk and sit on the edge of the alley, and Frank brings me some toilet paper from the bathroom to blow my nose.

I tell them the story.

"God, you guys. I'm really sorry," Frank says, shifting from leg to leg.

Skate scoots down the alley and cups my shoulder. "Rosie, I told you. I told you he's hopeless. Just completely hopeless. Now you *have* to believe it."

I look at her, look into her eyes that are just like his—eyes so blue and bright and alive—and I can see she really believes it's hopeless. I drop my chin to my chest and sob. I sob like I'll never stop.

"Listen to me, Rosie," Skate says, giving me a shake.

"Knock it off, Skate," Frank says.

He sits in the alley next to me holding the roll of toilet paper. He tears off sheets as my wad gets wet and crumpled. I dab at my runny eyes and nose and finally give myself the hiccups.

"I'm making your sister some homemade raviolis. I'm closing up soon. Come over and eat with us."

"Frank can cook," Skate pipes up.

I shake my head.

"This blows, for sure," Frank says. "But you still got to eat."

I shake my head and try to smile.

"Let's go outside," Skate says.

"Go easy," Frank whispers to Skate, poking her in the side.

We sit on a bench on the boardwalk overlooking the ocean. "Please don't give up on him," I whisper. Skate takes my hand but won't look at me. "Skate, do you think if Mom had lived, his life would be different?" *Mom.* How strange that sounds.

She looks at me, surprised. "Look," she says, "plenty of people lose a husband or wife and move on. Look at Julia. Perry's dad cheated on her—he couldn't keep it in his pants, if you know what I mean—and she was so hurt. She divorced him and now she's with Hal and she loves him. It must have been terrible for the Old Crow when she died. But still . . . Look at the sorry mess he's made. . . ." Skate slumps down on the bench. "That *sounds* so weird. *Mom.*"

We hardly ever talk about her. Here's what we know: when she died I was only one year old and just starting to take wobbly steps, and Skate was two and just starting to string words together. She died washing dishes. A blood clot traveled to her brain and killed her instantly. Snap your fingers. That fast.

"Skate, do you ever miss her?"

"It's hard to miss someone you didn't know." Skate speaks so low I can barely hear her.

"Why are you whispering?"

"I guess I don't want to hurt her feelings if she can hear us."

We both look up at the sky. It's dusk, the purple sky is darkening, and the waves hit the shore with a slap. "Skate, do you wish she was here right now?"

"That's wishing, not missing."

I nod, thinking about her, the slew of pictures we have. We got her high cheekbones, her long dark hair, her skinny legs, and even her love of lobsters in butter sauce. But I guess most people like lobsters in butter sauce.

"I just want to tell you something, Rosie." Skate turns away so I can't see her face. "I just want you to know that I think you and I are turning out fine. Despite all the bullshit—all the bullshitty bullshit—we're okay. You and me."

I try to smile. "Are you and Perry okay?"

Skates picks at the peeling paint on the bench. "It's so hard, Ro. Him there, me here. We're fighting a lot. Maybe it's just, you know, going to take some getting used to."

I nod, knowing they'll be all right.

"Come eat raviolis. You can roll out the dough. I'll make the filling."

I shake my head. "I want to talk to Gus or somebody."

Skate slouches down again. "I guess Drama Queen would be good for you at a time like this." She shivers and wraps her arms around herself. "Unbelievable, isn't it? The Old Crow."

I ride by Nick's house. I know I should give him space, like Angie says, but I can't help myself. I sit out in front of his house on my bike with my toes touching the stones, trying to decide what to do. Before I can decide, I push down my kickstand and walk to the kitchen window, where inside, Amy is pouring herself a glass of juice. I wave. "Hey, Rosie," she says, opening the door.

"Hey, is Nick around?"

She shakes her head.

"Do me a favor. Tell him I'm looking for him. Tell him it's about my dad."

"Sure."

"Be sure to tell him it's about my dad, not me."

She looks at me funny and says she will.

Gus lives on the north end of the bay. I'm not exactly sure where, so I ride the street looking for his beat-up car, but it's nowhere. I go to the deli and call him from a pay phone. His number has been sitting in my wallet ever since I started going to the meetings. But the phone rings and goes into voice mail. My voice chokes up so I can't leave a message.

When I walk into the kitchen, Angie's mashing potatoes. She's made stuffed peppers and even bought a mini lemon pie for dessert. But I'm barely hungry, and Angie lets me be quiet and pick at my food. She covers my plate with plastic wrap and sticks it in the refrigerator. When I try to wash dishes she tells me to take it easy. But I don't want to think about stuff, so I grab a towel and dry while she washes. Her rubber gloves squeak against the wet plates. "Do you think he'll get more time?" I finally say.

"He could, Rosie," she says, looking at me sadly. Later she asks me if I want to watch a movie about a boy werewolf. I tell her I'm tired.

In my room I sit at my desk with the phone by my side as I try to write a letter.

Dad, why did you do it? Don't you know you hurt all of us, not just yourself? Please tell me why.

I know the answer: he can't help it. But *why* can't he help it? I can see his battered old face crumpling. I know how sorry he'll be for letting everyone down, and I don't want to make him feel worse. I wad up the letter. The house is quiet except for the wind rushing at the glass in the windows. The phone is quiet too. "Come on," I say to it.

At midnight I head downstairs, ravenous. I heat up

my plate of stuffed peppers and mashed potatoes and green beans and wolf it down. Angie is asleep on the couch with the TV on.

There's a tap on the door. "Hey," Nick says, sliding inside when I open up.

"Hey," I say softly.

"Did something happen?"

I nod and the tears come again. "Let's go upstairs." We climb up to my room and sit on my bedroom floor. I mop my face with tissues as I tell Nick the story.

"That royally pisses me off," Nick says. "Selfish stupid bastard."

"Don't call him that, okay?"

"Come on, Rosie," he says, locking eyes with me. "Ah, I'm sorry." He takes an elastic out of his pocket and ties back his hair. His ears are flaming pink. "I'm really talking about my own lame-o dad when I say that."

I get more tissues and see in the mirror that my face is all wet and squishy pink and exhausted-looking. "Look at me," I say, half laughing, half crying.

"Poor Rosie. What a day you've had."

"Skate's totally given up on him," I say, sniffing.

He nods. "Maybe you should too."

I crawl onto my bed and look out the window, but it's a dark moonless night.

"Well, don't listen to me," Nick says. "You're more forgiving than me any day of the week."

I have such a bad headache from crying. I lie down

on my bed and close my eyes. "Thanks for coming by, Nick."

"Of course."

"Do you mind if I don't walk you out?"

"Can I stay for a little bit?"

"Okay," I say, opening my eyes. Nick lies next to me and reaches for my hand and holds it. His fingers are warm.

"Can I light that candle?" he asks.

"Uh-huh."

He lights a vanilla candle I have on my dresser and flips off the light. The room is chilly but bathed in warm light. Nick covers me with my quilt and slides in next to me.

"What could it be like?" I say. "Downing all those bottles of cough syrup?"

"How messed-up. How totally desperate."

"He must be so totally desperate. I bet if someone said 'Mr. Meyers, your life or a bottle of Vicks?' he'd take the bottle of Vicks."

"Yup," Nick says.

"How could he not care?"

Nick takes my hand again.

"I missed you," I tell him.

"Yeah, I guess we haven't seen each other much."

I wish he'd tell me why, but he doesn't. Soon my head stops hurting and I feel myself relax. Nick flips onto his side and touches my hair, running his fingers through it, making me feel all tingly. "I like your hair." And then he kisses my lips lightly. Barely. He waits a second and does it again. And then again. And when I open my eyes, he gives me a real kiss, a long kiss, and we wrap our arms around each other. It's so nice and cozy under the quilt with Nick that when he puts his hand under my shirt I don't stop him. And when he unhooks my bra I don't stop him. And when he unzips my jeans I don't stop him. It all happens so nice and slow. So nice and slow that I can stop thinking.

We're naked under the covers, our clothes pushed to the floor. "Do you have something?" Nick whispers.

"Do you mean—"

"A condom," he says. I reach into my drawer for the condom they handed out in health class last year. We figure it out in the candlelight, and soon Nick is inside me. Afterward, we look into each other's eyes, and Nick softly strokes my cheek. Don't close your eyes, Rosie, I tell myself. But they must grow heavy.

When I wake in the morning Nick is gone, and I am naked and there's a smear of blood between my legs. What have I done?

Skate

"You outdid yourself, Frank." I push away my plate and unbutton my jeans to let my stomach blub up and out.

Frank stabs the lone ravioli on his plate. "The gravy is a little blah." He eats it in one fast bite. "Salt, I think."

I shake my head. "It was de-lish." What a perfectionist he is.

"So, you going to tell your boy about the latest?" Frank asks.

I sigh and nod. "I'll see him in the morning."

Oh, Perry. He called early in the week and said he'd come home on Saturday to visit the Old Crow with me. Then he called the next day and said sorry, he couldn't. Then he called yesterday and said he might be able to, and that was when I got pissed. "Tell me right now. Yes or no. Either you are or you're not, dude." I was at Julia's, sitting at the kitchen table, painting my toenails.

"Skate, don't you see I'm trying here?"

"Yes or no?" I said.

"I guess not," he said. " 'Cause I'm not absolutely sure."

Yeah, I was mad about his wishy-washy flip-flopping, but it was hard to get too mad, because I don't want to visit the Old Crow anyway. And I must feel a little guilty, because I finally mailed off my letter. I even went to the post office to buy a stamp, because all Rosie had was LOVE stamps. I bought a ten-pack of wildflower stamps, and I chose a fluffy little weed for the envelope.

Last night Julia and I went to the mall, and she bought me a pair of dangly earrings. We didn't talk about Perry, but I know that she knows there's trouble. Then later as I stood in front of Perry's dresser mirror with my new earrings on, he called and said he wanted to see me and would definitely come home Sunday morning. He didn't sound wishy-washy. "I'll be there. I promise, Skate."

"Okay, then," I said, moving my head from side to side and watching my earrings flutter, wondering if I could really count on him.

The phone rings and Frank jumps for it. "Hey, you," he says, a big-ass smile breaking over his face. He shoos me away with his hand.

I grab a lollipop from his leftover bowl of Halloween candy and go out to the yard and sit in his rowboat. Frank really needs to settle down. I twirl the lollipop in my mouth. He should try dating the same girl for a year or so. He needs to fall in love like I did, the night of the bonfire last fall.

It was cold, the wind was raw, but the sky was filled with a million glittering stars. The fire crackled and popped and I stared into it, holding a plastic cup of beer from a keg. I'm not much of a drinker. I never get wasted. I only go as far as the warm glow. So I was glowing a little bit and looking into the flames when Perry plunked down next to me. "Skate," he said, his voice happy and warm in the cold night. "Here you are." We talked a little about all the usual things, but we were quiet too. It was fine just to be there on the sand, sipping beer and listening to the fire. Perry picked up a handful of sand and let it trickle through his fingers onto my hand. It made me shiver.

After that night we were together almost all the time. Some girls at school are always going through major dramas with their boyfriends. They cry in the bathrooms, have screaming matches in the courtyard, break up and make up and break up again, so that you can't keep it straight. Perry and I were never like that. Perry and I were *easy*.

Over the summer we were crabbing with drop lines in Perry's rowboat. I was leaning over the side, trailing my fingers into the water, and I said, "Per, we'll be to-gether forever, won't we." I didn't really say it like a question because I believed it.

"It's hard to imagine that couldn't be true," he said, shading his eyes from the sun and smiling at me. "But I wish you were older, Skate. I wish you were coming with me to Rutgers." I didn't wish that. I wished Perry was starting his junior year, like me. That way we'd have all this year and the next together. All that time. I never imagined it would be so hard, him going off to college. Missing Perry is like an ache. I keep rubbing my ache.

Frank opens the door and hands me my backpack and my board. "I have to throw you out. Sorry."

"Crap," I say. "Who is she?"

"A lovely dude, naturally, and she's coming over for a beer."

"Okay," I say, lifting myself out of the rowboat. "Have fun, Frank."

"I plan on it."

"Thanks for the raviolis."

"Yup. Besides, you should check on Rosie, you know."

"Are you laying a guilt trip on me?"

"She's pretty upset, Skate."

"I know."

But I don't want to think or talk about the Old Crow. So I ride up to Captain's Saloon on the board-walk. One of the bartenders is a friend of Frank's, so I don't think he'll throw me out. I take a seat at the bar, and Mikey leans down in my face. "What are you, like fifteen?"

"Sixteen going on seventeen, dude."

He gives me a cockeyed smile.

"Look," I say, rummaging in my backpack. "I only have a dollar. Will that get me a small Coke or something?"

He shakes his head but whisks a glass through a tub of ice and fills it with soda from a hose. "On the house," he says.

"Then this is your tip." I hand him the dollar, and he laughs and pockets it.

The bar is kind of depressing, I have to admit. There are some old men drinking by themselves. One is taking pieces of lint out of his pocket and lining them up on the bar. In the corner a hoochie mama is making out with some guy. A football game plays on the overhead TV.

"Frank treatin' you all right?" Mikey asks, swishing his rag across the bar.

"Frank's a good guy," I say.

"What's the story with you and Frankie, my man?"

"I work for him," I say, taking a sip. "He's my friend."

"Uh-huh," he says, like he doesn't buy it.

"Listen, Frank has enough girl trouble without me. Besides, I have a boyfriend."

"What are you doing here?"

"Killing time."

"Your boyfriend treatin' you all right?"

"Yup," I say. Not really, come to think of it.

I take out my history book and read a chapter about

the Treaty of Versailles. When the bar starts to fill up I decide to haul my butt over to Julia's. Perry will be here bright and early in the morning, if he's to be believed.

Julia's sitting up in bed reading. "Hey, Skate," she says.

"Hey." I linger in her doorway and try to decide if I want to tell her this latest business with the Old Crow. Part of me wants to, but a bigger part of me doesn't.

"You okay?"

I nod. "Just tired."

I take a long soak in the tub with Mr. Bubble. Julia has a slew of lavender bath beads, glittery liquids, and powdery flakes, which magically turn into foaming bubbles. When I'm puckered I wrap myself in a fluffy towel and go into Perry's room and stand naked in front of the dresser. I look at myself in the very same mirror Perry's been looking in all his life, and I have such a strange feeling then, looking at my long wet hair and slick skin, like maybe I don't belong here. I sit on the bed and look around the room. Our sweaters—the ones Perry didn't take to college—are heaped together on the closet shelf. My blue nail polish sits next to his Speed Stick. So why do I feel crappy?

I sleep late, I guess. Yawning, I walk into the kitchen, where Perry is already eating French toast. Julia's at the counter dipping slices of bread into raw eggs with cinnamon.

"Hey," I say, bending down to kiss him. "Why didn't you wake me?"

"I haven't been here long," he says, flashing his dark eyes up at me.

"But why didn't you wake me?"

He drags a piece of toast through a pool of syrup and holds it out for me to take a bite.

After breakfast, I'm getting dressed when Perry knocks on the bedroom door. He comes in and sits on the bed. I put on my new earrings and pile my hair on the top of my head, but Perry doesn't even seem to notice. "There's something I should tell you."

"I need to talk to you too."

"You first, then," I say, because I really don't want to tell him about this nasty business with the cough syrup.

We sit outside at the picnic table on the deck, looking out over the lagoon, which is as smooth as one of Julia's pressed sheets.

Perry gazes into my face like he wants to tell me something, but he doesn't say anything at all. He's so still that I feel a flutter in my gut. He starts to cry and lets his face fall into his hands. "Skate, I can't. This isn't working." He swipes at his wet eyes with his fingers. "It's too hard. I thought we could be together, but it doesn't work. And I met someone. I didn't mean to. . . ."

"Who?" I whisper.

"I'm so sorry, Skate. I don't want to hurt you."

The girl with the shiny hair. "Gina," I say.

"What?"

"You and Gina?"

"No, no. She's a friend. And you'll always be my friend, but this"—he waves his hand from me to him—"doesn't work anymore. It's too hard on both of us."

I blink. "You're breaking up with me?"

"I have to. I'm sorry. I just can't anymore." He touches my face and gets up and walks to his Hyundai.

"Where are you going?" I yell, running after him.

"Back to school."

"No!" I shout, grabbing the door, but he slams himself inside and starts the engine.

I bang on the window. "You can't, Perry. You can't!" He inches the car down the driveway. "Come back here!" I shout. "You come back!"

But he's in the street now, so I chase him until he outspeeds me. "The Old Crow got in trouble," I yell. "He's probably going—" But Perry's at the end of the block, and I watch the Hyundai get farther and farther away. I stand in the middle of the street until he's long gone.

Julia stands in front of the house with a dish towel. Blue polka dots. "Skate," she calls, and I can see right then that she knew this was coming. She knew why Perry came home. I grab my board and take off.

Rosie

I fake the flu. It's not hard, since I come down with a cold and I'm sneezing and a little stuffed-up anyway. I stay home one, then two days. Angie stands in the doorway on the third day. "Maybe you should go to school today, huh?" she says, throwing me a towel. "If you hurry you'll catch the bus."

"I don't know, Angie. I still have a fever." She presses the back of her hand to my forehead.

"Liar," she says. "Come on, Rosie, don't you need a change of scenery?" I scoot down farther into the blankets, liking the scenery right here, thank you. I sneeze right on cue. Angie shrugs.

Nick leaves a message, and when I don't call him back he shows up when I'm in my ratty robe reading a mystery under the covers. He sits cross-legged on my floor, kind of hunched over, and looks up at me. I clutch the robe to my neck and can barely breathe for some reason.

"You okay?" he asks.

"It's the flu or something." I fake a cough.

"I brought you some homework." He puts a pile of stuff on my bed.

"Hey, thanks." And then I feel funny in my ratty robe with dirty hair, so I pull the blanket over my head. "I must look a wreck."

"Honestly, you'd look fine if you washed that mop and ran a comb through it."

I peer out of the blanket, and Nick smiles at me, hooking his hair behind his ears.

"Are we okay, Rosie?"

I nod and glance out the window and feel myself grow warm, remembering his skin and my skin under this very blanket.

As if he read my thoughts, he says, "Are you sorry, Rosie?" He pulls on a thread in his holey jeans and sneaks a look at me. "About you and me? About what happened?"

"I don't know."

He looks away and blinks at my wastebasket. "I'm not sorry."

"It all happened so fast, Nick."

"We can slow down."

"Can we?"

He nods.

"I just have too many things in my head right now," I say.

Nick nods again and stands. "Will you call me soon?" I nod. He swings his backpack over his shoulder and reaches out his hand, but I'm afraid to touch him. So I don't, but he looks kind of hurt, his glance falling toward the rug. So I reach out an arm and lightly brush my fingers with his. He smiles, sort of. And then he's gone.

After he leaves, I take a shower and wash my mop and run a comb through it. I put on clean sweats and change my sheets and then crawl back into bed until my stomach starts to growl. Then I go downstairs and eat jelly toast and chicken soup and half a bag of chocolate-covered graham crackers. And three days home becomes four, then five. It's easy enough to do. And I don't call Nick.

Everything gets confusing. I ditch the meetings too. It's not Nick I'm avoiding. At least, I don't think he's the reason I don't go. It's just that I don't think it helps. Maybe Skate's right. When I don't show up, Gus leaves a message with Angie, but I don't call him back either. Then Julia calls, looking for Skate. But I haven't seen Skate in days. I just pretend like she's out.

Mostly I like being under the covers. I slide beneath the blankets, where it's dark and warm. I remember Nick's hands touching me and I lightly touch my bare stomach and give myself a shiver. It was nice, his fingers soft and gentle running up and down me, my fingers soft and gentle on him. But why can't I call him? Why don't I want to? Am I a normal girl? I hop out of bed and look at myself in the mirror, running my hands over my deeply flushed cheeks. I look like me still. But I'm not sure I'm me anymore. I'm different now, aren't I?

My feet get cold and I hunt in my sock drawer for my comfiest pair, and that's when I remember my summer job money, which was wadded up underneath the heap of socks. I remember discovering it was missing. I remember opening the drawer and there it wasn't anymore. "We've been robbed!" I cried, running into Skate's room. I dragged her into my room and showed her the drawer, filled only with socks.

"Yeah, you've been robbed, all right." She stormed downstairs, where our dad was passed out on the sunporch. She gave him a kick but he barely stirred. She kept knocking him around, but he was really out of it.

"He didn't," I kept saying, grabbing at her. She pushed me off.

"He did, Rosie. Grow the hell up."

When he wasn't so wasted the next day, Skate blasted him. "I borrowed it, Rosie girl," he said, looking at me with bloodshot eyes as he kneeled on the rug, sweeping his hand, looking for his sunglasses. "I'll pay you back," he croaked in a hoarse voice, spit forming in the corner of his mouth. Borrowed it. He borrowed it, I told myself. Relief made me feel like kneeling down next to him and hugging him. But I felt something else too. Something that made me feel like I was caving in on the inside. I didn't understand, though.

Now, as I touch my socks, I know. Of course I know. I imagine him coming into my room, uninvited, digging through each and every drawer until he discovers my stash of twenties, tens, fives, and ones buried beneath my furry blue socks. I imagine him lifting the wad of bills as if he had a right to, lifting the wad of bills and walking off. Walking off with what took me all summer to save.

The phone rings just then and I imagine it's him, calling me from the jail. "Hello!" I snap.

"Is Olivia there?" *Olivia?*

"Who is this?"

"I'll call back," the guy says, and hangs up.

Julia calls again, looking for Skate, and where is Skate if she's not at Julia's? Well, I can't know everything, now, can I? I take a message.

The weird guy calls the next day. "Olivia?" he says when I answer.

"You called yesterday, didn't you?"

"Who are you?" he asks.

"Who are *you*?" I say.

"Look. When can I reach her?"

"You can leave a message."

"Tell her Johnny called. Rutgers. Poker. You'll remember all that?"

"Johnny. Rutgers. Poker," I say. After he gives me his number, I hang up on him.

The end of the week, Skate comes flying in and sits on my bed. "Why are you ditching school? I ran into Nick. He says you haven't been there all week. I thought you were out only a couple of days. . . ."

I reach for a tissue and pretend to blow my nose.

"Rosie, there's nothing you can do about the Old Crow. So don't wallow in it. Get your butt to school."

"Who's Johnny?"

"Who?" she says, looking pissed.

I tell her and hand her his number. "My, my, my," she says.

"I have to tell you I don't like him. Is he a friend of Perry's?"

"Something like that. It's nothing," she says, stuffing the number in her pocket.

"Where have you been? Julia keeps calling."

"At Frank's." Skate takes a hair tie off my dresser and loops her hair into a ponytail and then gives her head a shake.

"Is something wrong, Skate?"

"Nothing that can't be fixed," she says.

"Tell me."

"Get your butt to school already."

"Tell me."

"I'll see you soon." And she flies out the door and dashes down the steps.

Saturday Julia calls a third time, and when I tell her Skate's out, she says, "Oh, shoot! I keep missing her. I'm kind of worried about her, Rosie."

" 'Cause of Perry?" I ask carefully. What could be wrong?

"How is she taking it?" Julia asks.

Could they have broken up? "Do you think . . ." I hold the phone cord tight as I scramble for the right words. "It's really over?"

"Yeah, I do," Julia says.

I hang up kind of stunned. But that can't be right, can it? I can picture Skate standing in front of my mirror, looping her hair into a ponytail. *My, my, my . . .* Now, does that seem like a person who's been dumped?

I get dressed—jeans, a sweater, sneakers—real clothes for a change—and ride my bike over to Lucky Louie's, where Frank sits behind the prize counter reading a textbook.

"Frank," I say, hurrying over. "Is Skate around?"

"I thought she was with you," he says, looking up from the book. "She blew off work, said she had a million things to do."

"What do you know about her and Perry breaking up?"

"What?" he says, pushing away the book.

I lean against the counter and tell him what I know. "I have the most rotten feeling she went to Rutgers."

"That girl," he says, shaking his head. "Could they really be kaput? She's definitely not acting like it."

We decide to drive to the train station to see if we can catch her. Frank puts on his Yankees cap backward and asks a friend of his in the pizza shop to watch the arcade. Then we climb into Frank's pickup and head over to Cove. But the train station's empty. I hop out of the truck and stare down the tracks at the misty darkness. Nothing.

"Why wouldn't she tell me?" Frank says when I climb back inside. "Why wouldn't she tell you?"

"Maybe she doesn't believe it's true. Maybe Perry ended it but she's not having it."

"Stubborn as they come." He shakes his head. "That girl."

"I can't even call her."

"Nope," Frank agrees. "So how are you doing, Rosie?" he asks as we head back to Mermaid. He fiddles with the radio and the classic-rock station crackles.

The question makes me bark out a laugh, because I don't know. I have no idea how I am. For a second I imagine saying to him: *My father's looking at more jail time. I slept with a boy for the first time and now I wish I could take it back.* Frank glances over at me, and I shrug and try to smile. Then I tell him how I've been holed up at home this week with a cold and how it's good, I guess, to finally be out of bed.

"Hey, you want to work a couple hours? I'll pay you to unload the prize boxes. Might be good to do something."

So we drive back to the boardwalk and for the next couple of hours I take inventory and separate yo-yos, SuperBalls, spider rings, whistles, spy glasses, and rub-on tattoos into bins. Then Frank gets us calzones and we sit at the counter and eat. Two senior girls from my school come into the arcade, snapping their gum and checking their cell phones. They wander over to the Love Meter. It's a romance tester and the picks are Uncontrollable, Passionate, Hot Stuff, Burning, Sexy, Wild, Mild, Harmless, Clammy, and Blah. The blond girl puts in money and squeezes the handle and each word lights up before it stops on Clammy. All of us laugh. After they leave, Frank boasts about how he never gets Clammy. "You probably jinxed yourself," I say, dipping my calzone in tomato sauce.

He takes the challenge and puts in fifty cents and the lights blink up and down the machine and land on Hot Stuff. "See," he says, cocking his head and grinning.

"You have this thing rigged?"

"Nah," he laughs. "I got Blah a couple times. Never Clammy, though."

Frank puts in two more quarters and tells me to give it a go. I squeeze the lever and get Burning.

"Not too shabby," he says, and I feel myself blush. *Burning.* Me.

"And Skate?" I say, scanning the words. "Wild, without a doubt."

"You said it, LD." Then he sings:

*"Wild thing
You make my heart sing."*

"What's 'LD'?"

Frank looks at me, surprised. "A lovely dude, naturally. LD for short." And I blush again.

He pays me forty dollars, which is a lot of money for a little over two hours, but when I stammer and try to hand it back he closes my fingers around the bills. "Take it, take it," he says. Then he offers to drive me home because it's cold and the wind has kicked up, but I want to ride.

"When you see Skate will you tell her to come see me?" I ask as I slip on my coat.

"Of course."

"I'm worried."

"Ah, she'll be okay."

"You think so?" I ask, looping my scarf around my neck.

He nods.

A curly-haired girl with big blue eyes comes sliding in and cocks her head at Frank. "Look, he's still alive!"

"Well, look who it is!" Frank says, beaming a smile at her.

"You were supposed to call me!" She folds her arms across her chest like she's mad, but she stands there smiling back at Frank.

He swoops behind her, like the Hot Stuff that he is, and wraps her in a big hug. "I totally was . . . but now here you are, LD." He whirls her around and kisses her, once, twice, three times, and she stops arguing with him. As I slip out, I turn back to see them making out in front of the fortune-teller machine.

Pedaling hard against the wind, I think about Nick and wonder if maybe he called me. But wasn't *I* supposed to call him? When I get home Angie says no, no call from Nick, so I call his house but the phone rings and goes into the machine. At the beep I want to say, *Nick, it's Rosie. I miss you.* But I can't. I just stand there with my heart pounding.

Skate

Maybe he's not so bad. Johnny, that is. *He's* going to meet me at the train station, which is more than *some* people would do. We're going to eat first—strombolis (his idea)—and then we're going to a party (my idea).

"You want to run into Perry, is that it?" Johnny said when I called him back late from Frank's kitchen while Frank was in the shower.

"I don't care if we do or if we don't," I said.

"Liar," he whispered. Then he laughed.

"Think whatever you want." The refrigerator hummed against my back.

"Look, a party's fine by me, Olivia."

"So that's our plan."

I don't know if I believe that Perry met someone. In any case, I don't care. Because whoever she is, she's not me. I have a whole year with Perry. A whole year of talking, walking, hanging, kissing, getting naked, laughing, surfing, crabbing, eating, working. Perry and I have all that, and you can't erase it. Here's what I'm thinking: Perry just needs a reminder of what's important. And I think I make a pretty good reminder. Showing up with Johnny might be an especially good reminder. When I catch my reflection in the train window, I'm smiling. I rest my head against the seat as the train whizzes past swamps and old warehouses with the windows knocked out and parking lots full of trucks. The moon is bright in the sky as the train chugs along, bringing me closer to Rutgers.

I almost told Frank everything this morning. He was a grouch, though, hunched over his Cocoa Puffs. Said he had a sore back because his latest LD—the one who came over for a beer last week—has a miserable bed, all mushy in the middle. So he was kind of giving me the evil eye.

"I guess you'd rather sleep in your own bed," I said, wadding up the sheets and blue blanket. He grunted something as I gave the couch pillows a slap to puff them back up. "I'll leave, Frank. Look, I don't want to be a pain in the butt."

"The thing is," he said, "I can't exactly bring her home with you on the couch." And then he looked kind of guilty as he slurped down a milky spoonful of cereal.

"I get it. Really, it's okay." And I thought then of telling him what happened with Perry, but I thought he might feel sorry for me, and I don't want him feeling sorry for me, because things aren't what they seem, and I'm probably the only one who realizes it.

Johnny is late. I stand outside the train station until I get too cold, then I go inside and sit on a bench. Every few minutes I check outside. Oh, why don't I have a cell phone! Makes me so mad. I get tired of waiting and call Perry's cell from a pay phone, but it goes right to voice mail. Hearing his voice gives me a pang, and I can't seem to hang up. Then I feel a tap on my shoulder. It's Johnny, looking cool in a corduroy jacket and dark jeans.

"Hey. You're late," I say, hanging up the phone.

"What, like ten minutes?" He cocks his head and pushes his feathery hair out of his eyes as he checks me out. Slowly, he smiles. "So are we going to have fun, or are you going to give me a hard time?"

I look at the clock hanging above the ticket booths. He's a half hour late. "I'll start having fun when you give me a reason to."

"Listen to you," he says. "Hey, I'm sorry. I lost track of time. Are you hungry?" I nod.

We go this stromboli place, which is packed with kids. The place is dark and noisy and reeks of beer. We squeeze into a tiny booth and when we order, Johnny gets a pitcher of beer. The waiter cards him, and he shows him an ID.

"Pretty slick," I say. "Where'd you get that?"

"Oh, it's not hard." It doesn't take long until a bus-boy plunks down Johnny's pitcher. Foam sloshes over the side. Johnny grins and pours us glasses. My Coke never comes. The place is busy and we have to swipe silverware and napkins off another table because our waiter is nowhere to be found. It's so loud that we have to shout, and Johnny's phone keeps ringing and each time he takes the call. Meanwhile I finish off my beer, and Johnny gives me a refill. The third time I put my hand over the glass, but he laces his fingers through mine, and with his other hand he refills my glass.

"Slick, dude," I tell him. But his phone is ringing again, and he doesn't hear. I look around for Perry, but I don't see him. Rutgers is a big place, and I have the terrible feeling that he may not be at the party either. The food takes forever, but I've got a glow on, so I don't mind.

Johnny tells me he'll be right back, and I ask to borrow his cell. "You need to get your own," he says.

Duh. I call Perry's phone again, and again it goes into his message. Listening to his voice—*You got me. I'll call you back*—makes me miss him in the worst way. Oh, Perry!

"Sorry, sorry," Johnny says, sliding back into the booth. "A million things going on." I must have drained my glass, because he quickly refills it.

"I'm done," I tell him, pushing it away. He smiles.

Our waiter flings our strombolis at us. They're steaming hot and as big as our heads. Food always makes me happy, so I chow down. I only sip the beer but then that glass is empty too.

Johnny pays, and it isn't until I stand that I realize I have more than a warm glow going. I'm a little drunk as I stumble out onto the sidewalk. I wiggle my fingers, 'cause even they feel a little bit drunk. First stop is a friend of Johnny's, a big messy house with a living room full of people. A joint is passed around, but I don't like to smoke, so I shake my head. Johnny makes a face. "Suit yourself."

"I always do." But I smile when I say it, and Johnny tells me I'm a handful, which makes me roll my eyes. Someone gives me a bottle of beer and I sip it. No one talks to me, which is okay, I guess. I wander into the kitchen and sit at the table. The place is a mess, with a sinkful of tomato-sauce-crusted dishes. I don't mean to drink the whole beer, but I guess I do. There's a phone on the wall and I call Perry's cell. This time he answers. "Hello . . . hello." There's noise on his end, and the noise from the living room floats into the kitchen, and I almost blurt out *It's me.* He says something to whoever he's with, but I don't catch it. Then he hangs up.

I let Johnny sling an arm over my shoulder when he whisks me out into the cold. "How about that party?" I say.

"And what was *that*?"

"*That* was lame."

"The night is young, Olivia." Oh, how I hate him calling me Olivia. "Why don't we dump your board in my dorm?"

"I can take it with me."

"You'll lose it."

"Haven't lost it yet." But he gets his way, and we stop at his dorm room, which is just like Perry's. I lean my board against his closet. "Okay, let's go."

"Sit for a minute," he says. I give him a look. "Come on." So I sigh and plunk myself on his desk chair. "So how does a high school girl get to stay out all night long?"

"I just do."

"No one breathing down your neck? A nagging mom, a clock-watching dad?"

"My mom died, my dad doesn't care."

He opens his minifridge and cracks open a beer. He hands it to me, but I shake my head. He shrugs and takes a drink. "Sorry about your mom."

"I was a baby. I don't even remember her. You know, she's an *idea,* not a person to me. That sounds mean, but it's true."

He shrugs. "It makes sense."

"The thing is," I say louder than I mean to, "I just don't know what to think about her. I never have."

Johnny looks at me.

"I mean, you said 'sorry,' and it's sad in theory, but what am *I* supposed to feel? Who is this person? *Mom?* Who? You see?"

"Are you wasted?" Johnny laughs, his mouth stretching wide.

"I'm something." I lift my legs onto the bed. Johnny hands me the beer, and—what the heck—I take a long sip.

"You wearing that purple bra?"

"Wouldn't you like to know?"

"Yeah, I would." He laughs, and I do too. "Kiss me, Olivia."

"I don't feel like it." I take another sip and beam a smile on him. "I mean, I don't feel like it right now." I'll give him hope. Why the freak not?

"Too wasted to make out?"

"I can make out, dude."

"Prove it."

"Nice try."

"You never asked why I called you," he says.

"Tell me, then."

"Brockner dumped you."

I cock my head and stare him down. "It's a little more complicated than that."

"It always is." And he smiles. "I'm happy to see you, you know." He pats the mattress, so I sit next to him on the bed. "I'm glad you came." He buries his nose in my hair. "You can do better than Brockner. That wimp."

"Wishy-washy maybe," I say. "But he's not exactly a wimp."

"Wishy-washy. Wimp. Wuss. Same thing." And for some reason it's funny. Really funny, and we laugh into each other's faces. Ha ha ha. I grab his beer and take a long sip. Then I lie back on the bed, close my eyes, and the room spins gently gently gently, and this is kind of funny too. I laugh and Johnny curls up next to me. *Wimp.* I laugh again. *Wuss.* I can hear Perry—college-boy Perry: *I have sooo much work. I'm freaking! I'm trrrying.* Then whip-fast, I'm totally fed up with him, but it's sort of funny too. I giggle, and let Johnny kiss me. I kiss him back. Just this once. It won't count. Not really. His mouth is wet. Too wet. Not like Perry's. He doesn't kiss like Perry at all. But Perry is a wuss. A wimp. A wussy boy.

Johnny gives me a wet kiss on the cheek. "Do you know who wussy boy is with these days?"

"Gina," I say, bracing myself.

"Oh, please. You mean you don't know? Oh, you got to get a load of this," Johnny says, sitting up. "Come on."

3:10 a.m.

My fingers keep missing the numbers, and I dial again and again. Finally, but it rings and rings. I fumble with my sweater, trying to get my arm in the sleeve. Then Frank's voice mail. "Frank!" I yell. "Frank!" Nothing. I hang up and call again. My fingers miss. Finally.

"Skate?" Frank says, sleepy-voiced.

"Frank, help me."

"Skate! What happened?"

And then I do something I never do. I cry. "Frank . . ." The tears drip down my face. "Frank. Come get me."

"Tell me where you are."

"I don't know."

"Are you drunk?"

"I don't know."

"Are you at Rutgers?"

"Yes."

"Can you get to the train station? I can meet you there. It's gonna take me about an hour and a half." I hear someone's voice, and then Frank's whisper.

"The station is closed. It's cold out, Frank."

"Listen to me. Head over to the train station, okay? There's probably a diner or something open. Wait there. It's three-eleven. I'll be there be, like, four-thirty. So at four-thirty head over to the train station. Okay, Skate?"

"Frank . . ."

"Say it back to me. Say what I just said."

I say it back.

"Okay, good," he says. "Four-thirty train station."

"Frank, he loves someone else. Perry loves someone else."

"Do you have money for a cup of coffee?"

"Uh-huh." I sniff.

"Go have a cup of coffee. Eat something too. It'll soak up some of that beer. Is that what you were drinking? I'll be there soon."

It's cold enough to see my breath, but I don't feel cold. I stumble over a crack in the sidewalk. Sleep. Home, please. But where is home, anyway? I follow some kids and here is a street I know. There's the diner from last time. I head in and fall into a booth and put my head on the paper place mat. The table smells like ketchup.

"Hey, are you going to be sick?" the waitress says.

"No," I say, lifting my head. "Coffee and a muffin."

"What kind of muffin?"

"I don't know."

"Blueberry, banana, carrot, chocolate chip . . ."

"Yes," I say.

"You have money?"

I pull five dollars out of my pocket, and she walks away. The coffee comes and it's nasty, so I drown it in milk, then sugar. The waitress comes with a plate of muffins. "Point," she tells me. I point to the chocolate one.

"Don't drink so much," she scolds me.

I push my hair off my face. "Can you tell me when it's four-thirty?"

"You don't have a watch?" I shake my head, and she sighs.

I lean my head against the cold window and chew slowly. Every now and then I bite into a gooey chip and it tastes so good I want to cry all over again.

There were a lot of people. There was a keg, so we drank some more. A couch. We sat on a couch. There were shots. Kamikazes. Like gasoline down my throat. Johnny kept grabbing me, making me kiss him. It was like a joke, then it wasn't. We wandered through rooms, and then I saw him. Perry and that blond girl. That blond girl—the nice one who's as plain as a potato. *Her.* Perry had his arm around her. She drank out of a straw and twirled it around her cup, smiling up at Perry. When she smiled she wasn't so plain. Not really. She smiled right into his face. She did. He smiled right into hers. Then he kissed her, slowly, nicely. I watched, and Johnny watched me watch. "Brockner, that wuss," he whispered in my ear. "Eleanor is about as hot as a cold piece of pizza." From across the room, I watched them laugh together. Oh, how many times I've seen Perry's happy face. She tilted her plain blond head up to his and he smiled down at her. Then he gathered her up in his arms and they were making out. And when they stopped, they stayed in a hug. A long hug. Perry kissed her hair. How many times has he kissed my hair? So many times. Johnny poked me. "Let's give him something to look at." Johnny crammed his tongue into my mouth.

"Stop," I said. But it was hard to stand, so I leaned against him. "Let's sit, Johnny." But there was nowhere to sit. Johnny pulled me upstairs, weaving in and out of kids sitting on the steps. I kept falling against him. Upstairs, he pulled me into a bathroom. I sat on the rim of the tub and put my head between my legs and grew dizzy. Johnny sat down next to me and put his arm around me. "Don't crash on me now."

"Let's leave."

"Kiss me."

"I don't feel so good."

"Don't be a baby." He rammed his hand underneath my sweater. "Let me see that purple bra."

"Get off." But he held me tight, and I couldn't break away. I felt as light and weak as a kitten. And together we sank to the dirty yellow rug on the bathroom floor. He yanked my sweater over my head. Did I yell? I think so. He unhooked my bra. And there I was half-naked in front of some boy I don't know and don't like. While downstairs a boy I loved was loving some other girl. Johnny touched me and squeezed me and ran his hands all over me, kissing me with that wet mouth, while I squirmed and tried to push him away. Someone banged on the door and when Johnny half turned, I grabbed my sweater and pushed past him and ran out half-naked past two boys. I ran to the end of the hall and into a bedroom, and that's where I found a phone. Shaking and fumbling with my bra, I dialed Frank.

At four-thirty the waitress points to her watch. I leave her the five dollars. It's still dark as I hurry to the station, and there's Frank's pickup by the curb. He gets out of the truck, and I run, plowing into him. I think I'll cry, but I don't. Frank wraps his arms around me.

"Are you okay?"

I nod. "My board's in this guy's room. I need my board."

"What guy?"

"Just this guy." Then I burst into tears.

"Did he hurt you?"

I wave my hand. "My board, Frank."

"Did he touch you?"

I cover my mouth with my hand.

"I'll kill him."

"My board, Frank. Just get it."

We drive to the dorm. I know the way. Frank bangs on Johnny's door. "Open up," he says. "Now." I can hear him inside. "Dude, open the door or I'm knocking it down." Johnny, half-asleep in a T-shirt and pajama bottoms, swings open the door. "Give me the skateboard," Frank says.

Johnny hands it over, eying me the whole time. "You baby. Go back to high school."

"I should knock you out," Frank says. I give Johnny the finger.

We don't say much, me and Frank. He plays the classic-rock station on low. When we get back to Mermaid, he drives straight to his house and makes up the couch with sheets and the soft blue blanket, and he gets the pillow from the hall closet.

"I'm so sorry, Frank," I whisper.

"I'm sorry too," he says, glancing at me.

I crawl between the sheets and feel dizzy when I close my eyes, as if none of this is real. And maybe when I wake up it won't be.

"Frank," I say.

"Go to sleep, Skate."

"I can't."

"Shhh . . ."

"Don't tell me to shush."

"I just did. Go to sleep."

"I can't."

"Yes, you can. Shhh . . ."

"Shut up, Frank!" I yell, as if he's the one I'm mad at.

"What the hell did you think you were doing?" Frank yells back, looming over me. "You don't seem to know it, but you're still a kid. Look at me. You had no business up there. None at all."

"Don't get all high and mighty with me," I yell.

"Look, that pig could have . . . Look, you don't know jack squat about the world."

"Like you do! You can't keep a girlfriend. You go

through them like M&M's. *I* had a relationship. For a whole year. I was with Perry for a whole year. I had . . . I had . . ." But then I start to sob, really sob. Frank sits on the edge of the couch while my eyes and nose run so I'm a runny mess. Even my hair gets wet. When I catch my breath, I give him a shove. "What do you know about love?"

"I know a thing or two, Skate," he says softly.

"I'm sorry." I curl up into a ball, wetting the sheet with my cheek. I grab Frank's wrist. "Perry loves someone else, he loves someone else." When I close my eyes, the room spins in a slow dreamlike way. "He loves someone else."

"Be quiet, LD. Let me take care of you." Frank pulls me onto his lap and holds me.

"He loves someone else," I whisper again and again.

We stay like that for a long time. Our breathing sinks us deeper and deeper into the cushions. Frank smells like sleep and I curl against him, wishing for sleep to come to me.

Rosie

"It's Gus," Angie mouths, her hand over the phone. I shake my head. "Come on," she whispers. Angie looks at me unhappily, but I'm not budging. I dig into my apple pie. "Uh, sorry, she's not here. Can I have her call you? Okay. Bye." She hangs up and slides into a seat next to me. "You going to eat all that?" I shake my head, and she stabs a piece with a fork.

"What did he want?" I ask.

"What do you think? Why'd you stop going to those meetings?"

" 'Cause they don't help."

"Come on, Rosie . . ."

I pick at a bit of crust. "I have to believe in it, and I don't right now."

"Gus sounds nice. Is he?"

I smile, just thinking of him. "He is."

"Is anything weird going on with you and Nick?"

I push the plate toward her, and she digs in. "No, why?"

"I don't know. He doesn't come over as much."

I wish I could tell Angie, but I can't. Not that.

"All right, girly girl. We're just going to call you the Clam," she says in a mobster voice. "The Clam never gives anything away." I smile and roll my eyes. The phone rings again, and for a second I sort of hope it *is* Nick.

"Uncle Harry. Hi!" Angie says, her eyes growing wide. Not my father! I shake my head back and forth very fast. "Rosie . . . well, let me see. Hold on." She covers the mouthpiece and looks at me pleadingly. "Rosie," she whispers, "he's lost his visiting privileges. This is all you're going to get." And I shake my head very slowly this time. "Just say hi?" she urges.

No way. I climb up to my room and hang out the window, looking at the sea. My hair whooshes crazily around my head. It feels good to be angry at him, and these days I can get angry at him in an instant when I think about the money in my sock drawer, the cough syrup, his promises, his bottles of Old Crow . . . so many things.

Soon Angie comes in and plops down beside me. Her Cleopatra hair blows against my cheek. She smells like cinnamon and strawberry lip gloss. "Dang. It's cold," she says after a while. I shut the window, and we shiver together on my bed.

"God, Rosie," she says, throwing my quilt over her

shoulders. "You're doing what I did. . . . You know, when everything happened with your dad, and my father called me and asked if I might come up and stay with you guys, I just jumped at the chance. I left everything, including my boyfriend."

"You didn't tell me you had a boyfriend."

"Well, I did. We were having problems. Fighting a lot. He'd say maybe we should break up. I'd say yeah, maybe we should. But then we wouldn't. He's a flirt. He likes to be out and about. And me—you know, I like to stay home, cook, rent movies, hang out. I guess we weren't much of a match, but I loved him—maybe I still love him." She sighs and curls up on my pillow. "When I got the call from my father, I fled. I sublet my apartment in about ten minutes' time, took a leave from my salon, loaded up my car, and I was off to New Jersey. I didn't even say goodbye to Steve. I left a Post-it note on his windshield. Nice, huh?"

"You should call him."

"I know! Why don't I? Because I'm a big fat chicken. I don't want to deal with the mess. I figure he's pissed and will blow me off."

"You don't seem like a chicken."

"Well, I am."

"So I guess you're saying I'm a big fat chicken too," I say, hanging my head over the edge of the bed.

"I'm not saying anything, girly girl," she says, giving me a friendly kick in the shin.

The doorbell rings. It's a big old-fashioned chime that echoes loud through the walls. We look at each other. Hardly anyone ever uses the front door. We all come and go through the kitchen. Angie rolls off the bed. "I don't suppose you'll scurry down there and get it? You're younger and skinnier and faster."

So I take my young, skinny, fast self and dash downstairs, knowing at least it won't be Nick standing there. He'd rap on the kitchen windowpane. It takes two hands to open the creaky door, and there stands Gus, smiling and glad to see me.

"Gus!" I say happily. I kind of throw myself at him and we wind up in a hug.

"Rosie, hello."

"You want to come in?" He nods. I take him into the kitchen and tell him to have a seat while I open the cabinets and get busy making us hot chocolate.

"What a great old house," he says.

"It is. But it's kind of coming apart at the seams. It's dark now so you probably can't tell." I lick at the whipped cream, feeling fluttery with Gus sitting across from me.

"Why'd you stop coming?" Gus looks at me all serious. His eyes are very pale—maybe gray or green—under the kitchen lights.

I shrug.

"Come on, tell me. I know about the latest with your dad."

"I've been busy, Gus."

"Doing what?" he says, slurping his drink.

"Stuff."

"What kind of stuff?"

"Hey, want the grand tour?" I ask, putting down my cup. "Want to see the house?"

"Okay, why not." So I start on the first floor, taking Gus into all the rooms, even the ones we don't use, like the main living room. I bet if we were to sit on the threadbare couch a cloud of dust would puff into the air. I even take him into the funny little room with all the hooks on the wall. Then we go the second floor and I show him the big bathroom with the fancy claw-foot tub. Then I show him the front sleeping porch. It's long and narrow with six cots. My dad and uncle and their cousins used to sleep here in the summer when they were kids, and Skate and I liked it when we were little. I don't think those cots have been used in years. I point to my dad's room and then Angie's. Soft light and the song "What a Wonderful World" seep out the bottom of her door.

I see skies of blue, clouds of white
Bright blessed days, dark sacred nights . . .

We stand for a minute in the half-dark, listening, and when our eyes meet we smile at each other. We head up to the third floor then, where I throw open my door and Skate's, so he can see our views of the ocean. And I take him into the junk room, loaded with all kinds of furniture, crappy stuff and antiques too. Sometimes I like to come in here to think. Now I sit on an end table in front of the window. A few boats hover on the bay, moving slowly through the fog. Gus sits on a wobbly Adirondack chair across from me and grins as it teeters from side to side. There's no electricity in the room, so I strike a match and light the candle I keep in here, and we look at each other across the flame.

"Tell me what's wrong," he says.

"Everything," I say.

"Tell me."

I shake my head.

"Please."

It's the way he says *please,* so soft and quiet. So nice. His pale eyes fixed on me, above the candle. I scramble over to him and kneel with my hands on his knees. "Oh, Gus," I say. He puts his hands over mine; they're warm and big. "Will everything always be so hard? Will it?" I ask, my voice breaking.

"I don't think so, Rosie."

"What if he never stops drinking?"

"Then he never stops drinking."

"What if he gets thrown in jail again?"

"Then he gets thrown in jail again."

"What if he dies?"

"Then he——"

"Don't." I push away and sit on the floor, and Gus slides off the chair and joins me.

"I didn't mean that," he says. And I throw my arms around him and bury my face in his warm neck. I kiss him right then, right on the lips, and feel his surprise, feel him tighten up, so I pull away and wrap my arms around my legs.

"Do you like me?" I ask, staring at my knees.

Gus tries to tip my face toward his, but I don't let him. "I like you very much."

I close my eyes, understanding. "As a person? As a friend?"

"Yes."

"You have a girlfriend?"

"Anita. That's her name. I met her at a meeting. She's in college too."

"Anita," I say, trying to picture her. "Is she easy to talk to?"

"Yeah."

"Is she your best friend?"

"She is."

"Is she pretty?"

He laughs softly. "Well, I think so."

"Blonde or brunette?" I sneak a look at him. "Sorry, I just want to picture her."

"She has black hair. Long hair. She's West Indian."

"And someone in her life's a drunk?"

"That's right."

"How do you like that," I say quietly.

"Yep," Gus says. "How do you like that." I take a deep breath, feeling damp and warm and strangely dizzy. Gus stands and slides back into the wobbly Adirondack chair. I lean my head against his knee.

"My father called," I say. "I won't talk to him. I can't."

"Good."

"So this is what it means to let go. Still . . . I can't help thinking that if I really let go everything will come crashing down."

"Nope. The truth is you're not holding it up. Let him sink or swim. It's his butt on the line. He's got to sink or swim."

"Sink or swim."

"Yep."

"Okay."

I don't want to move—not yet—so we sit there with the flame flickering and the wind rattling the window.

"How do you take something back, Gus?"

"What do you mean?"

"Let's say," I whisper, "you did something you didn't mean to do and now everything feels ruined. Can you take it back?" On the bay, a lone boat heads home to the marina, its lights blurred in the mist.

"I don't know . . . ," Gus says, running his hand over my hair.

"Come on."

"What are we talking about?"

But I can't tell him that. "Come on," I say, glancing up at him. "Can you take something back?"

"Do you think I know everything?"

"Mostly," I say. "Don't you?"

"Oh, please . . . ," he says, smiling down at me. "We're talking about Nick, aren't we?" But I can't answer that. I *can't*.

It isn't until midweek that I finally catch up with Skate. At lunchtime at school. She's sitting alone outside at a table, drinking apple juice. And I can tell from looking out the window at her that it's over with Perry. I can see it in every inch of her. It's the way she's so still, like a statue—Skate, who's always in motion. As if she hears me, she sweeps her hair off her face and takes a sip of juice.

"Hey, where have you been?" I ask, hurrying over to her.

"I must have caught what you had."

"Is it true about you and Perry?" I say, joining her on the bench.

"I can't talk about that here."

So after school we ride the bus together, and we hop off in the Heights. At first I think we're going to hang out at the arcade, but we walk along the boardwalk with seagulls squawking over our heads. Captain's Saloon is mostly empty. We sit at the bar and order Cokes.

"So tell me, Skate."

"I'll live," she says.

"Don't be like that."

"I'm just saying."

"I'm really, really sorry," I say.

"Will you quit being sorry?" She crunches furiously on an ice cube.

"Don't be so tough," I say. "Could it just be that you guys need some time to work it out?" Skate shakes her head, and I grow warm and shaky. "Well, I feel terrible about it. I do. I really do. I like Perry, and I liked you and him together, and I'm just so . . ." Skate stares at me, her eyes wide and blank. "I'll shut up, then," I say. She drops her head into her hands and rubs her face and gives me such a tired-out smile that I almost want to cry. "Oh, Skate," I say, touching her arm.

"So what's going on with you?" she says, shrugging me off.

"I slept with Nick," I blurt out.

"You?"

"What do you mean *me*?"

She shakes her head. "I didn't mean it like that."

"Well, we did, and now I just don't know. I just don't know."

During fourth period I stared at the back of his head

in geometry, willing him to turn around so I could smile. But he didn't. Then after class, he waited for me in the hall, leaning against the wall. "Hey," he said as I walked out.

"Hey," I answered, but then I couldn't think of a thing to say and we walked to our next classes like two mutes, the silence between us so loud it filled my ears like wet cement.

"Well, do you like him?" Skate asks.

I nod.

"So it'll be okay."

I shake my head. "I kind of wish I could take it back. . . ."

"Was it bad?" Skate whispers.

"What do you mean bad?"

"Was he all fumbling? Was it *not* nice?"

"It was nice, but . . . oh, something must be wrong with me." I twirl my straw in my Coke. "I can't explain."

Skate sizes me up. "It sounds like it was too fast. You weren't ready yet. Tell him. That's all."

"Then what?"

"What do you mean then what? So you kiss and fool around but you don't go all the way unless you want to."

"You make it sound easy." She stares back at me, not understanding. "You only get one first time, right?" I ask.

"Just slow it down, Rosie," Skate says nicely, her hand resting on my knee. "It'll be okay."

"Hey, girls," Mikey says, swinging through the kitchen door. "Hard day at school? Needed to throw back a couple of shots?"

"Ha ha," Skate says.

"I just like to bust your chops," he says to her.

"We don't need our chops busted, dude." She shoos him with her hand. "So take your chop-busting—"

"Ah, I'm just teasing. God, you two are gloomy," he says, checking us out. Skate makes a face. "Well, I've got my own woes. You know anybody who wants a puppy?"

"Who has a puppy?" Skate asks, perking up.

"I do. Two." Mikey carries an air conditioner box out of the kitchen. "My dog got knocked up and I'm really pissed off about it. So now I have Jelly plus these two. I gotta find homes or they're going to the pound."

"The pound!" Skate yells.

"Hey, chill. They're puppies. Somebody'll take them. And get this: Jelly developed a nipple infection. *A nipple infection.* My *dog.* Which is why she's at the vet's and which is why I'm babysitting. And which is going to cost me like two hundred bucks. Boy, am I pissed off."

"Let's see the puppies," Skate says, hanging over the bar, looking flushed and happy.

"Yeah, all right." Mikey plucks up a little black ball from the box and thrusts it at me. When I cup my hands under it, it whimpers, and I jump. I hand it off to Skate and she lifts its little face to hers, the rest of it dangling from her hand. "Hi, pupster," she says.

"They just started hopping around and wagging their tails," Mikey says. "Before their eyes opened they were just these amazingly sleepy creatures. They still sleep a lot. Man, what a life."

Skate takes the puppy and sticks it down the front of her sweater. Its drowsy little face rests on her top button. She pets the top of its head with a finger.

"Careful," I say. "It might pee."

"How much pee could it have?" She laughs. "Look at it." The puppy yawns and seems to sigh. "When can I have them?" she says to Mikey.

"Skate!" I say.

"Soon," he says, lighting up.

"Frank'll never go for it," Skate says to me. "But I bet Angie would be cool. It's not like they're going to mess up the house." We laugh.

"You'll move home, then!" I say, suddenly as flushed and happy as she is.

Skate

❧

I didn't think I could take it. But I'm taking it. Somehow. It's bright and warm today, more like an early fall day than November. So I ride over to the house and get my surfboard and wet suit out of the shed. The waves are decent too, and while I'm riding I see Julia walking over the sand, her red hair flaming under the sunny skies. I called her back. Eventually I did. There wasn't much to say. "Promise you'll stop by?" she asked.

"Yeah," I said, though I haven't yet. She even dropped off a tray of macaroni and cheese with the crunchy top. Angie called me at the arcade to tell me. Angie's figured out my situation—me staying at Frank's— and she cornered me as I heated up some mac 'n' cheese.

"How about moving home, Skate?"

I shrugged.

"You've got a nice bed upstairs and you should use it. Rosie misses you, you know."

I smiled but kept my trap shut. I don't want to tell

her about the puppies and my plans to bring them home just yet.

Julia comes to the water's edge and squats down, shielding her eyes. I ride a few more waves, and then I let myself coast in. I stick my board in the hard wet sand and drop down next to her.

"How's the water?" she asks, glancing up at me.

"Really good today."

"I like watching you. How come you don't crash on the slow waves?" She laughs. "You have a flair for slow-motion surfing."

"I crash sometimes," I say.

"Yeah, of course."

I take off my hood and push away the few strands of wet hair clinging to my face and neck.

"I really think this is a good thing, Skate." She squints as if it hurts her to say it. "Perry was off having adventures, and it was like you were on hold. I hated to see you on hold."

She's only trying to make me feel better. I know that. I take off my booties and bury my feet in the cold sand. "I'll never meet anyone I like as much as Perry."

"That's only because you haven't met him yet."

"There are some real jerks out there, Julia." I don't mean to cry, but lately I've got the waterworks going—not sobbing, exactly, but a lone tear slides out and rolls down my cheek. I let my hair fall in front of my face to hide it. We're quiet, and this is what I like about Julia.

Some mom types might take an opportunity like that to grab you, plant a kiss on you, and tell you how special you are or some crap. But Julia just sits with me while I pull it together. Soon my eyes are dry, and I look up, wipe my nose. "Is he happy . . . with his new girlfriend?"

"He hasn't said much. Honestly."

"Do you think I bugged Perry too much about the Old Crow? Always complaining about him . . ."

"Everyone has problems, kiddo. Don't think that."

"Not everyone has a father in jail."

Julia clasps my knee. "You'll stop missing Perry so much."

"Maybe I don't want to," I say. "Did you ever think of that?" I don't mean to get so pissy, but I feel myself heat up. What does Julia or anyone know about it? How can anyone know what it was like between us?

"You're absolutely right," Julia says, looking out over the waves. "Maybe you're not ready to—"

"Oh, humor me!" I hop to my feet and grab my board. "That's good. . . ."

"Skate, if I could think of one darn thing to make you feel better I would do it in a second."

"Well . . . you can't," I say softly.

Julia stands and wipes sand from her butt. "Stop over Thanksgiving weekend and see us, will you? Perry'll be home."

"Maybe." But I don't think I can.

✻

I visit the puppies every day—there's a girl and a boy. Mikey even gives me a key, so if he's working I can stop over. When the puppies see me they jump up on the sides of the makeshift pen, their eyes bright, their tails wagging. When I let them out, they race in laps around the room, stopping now and then to hop on me with their little paws. Jelly's much more laid-back. She strolls over and gives me a sniff and a lick while the pupsters dance and leap beneath her.

I named them after the lighthouses—Old Barney on the north end of the island and Lorry Lee off the south. So Barney and Lorry it is.

One sunny day, I take Jelly, Barney, and Lorry to the beach. The puppies are a little shy at first, because it's their first good look at the big wide world. "Go," I tell them as they stare up at me. "Have a look around. Explore." And after they get the hang of the sand, they're soon chasing each other around and jumping into the air after seagulls. But, funny enough, they won't put their little butts on the sand. After they wear themselves out, which doesn't take long, they pile onto my lap.

Usually I visit the puppies after school and then head over to the arcade, if I'm working, or Frank's place to do homework, if I'm not. Sometimes I go to the house and hang out with Rosie and Angie. I still haven't told Angie about the puppies—about my plan to bring them over—but I'm not worried.

I tell Frank, though. We're sitting on the couch eating

vanilla ice cream and watching a rerun of *Scrubs* when I tell him that Mikey said I can have the puppies tomorrow after he brings them to the vet. "So I'll clear out then."

"Where you going?" Frank asks, putting down his bowl.

"Back to the house."

"Really? Why?"

"Well, I didn't think you'd let me have two puppies."

"I just figured you'd bring them here."

"You did? But I figured you'd never go for that."

"Look," he says, taking off his Yankees cap and scratching his head. "Why not? Besides, I like dogs and they like me. But you're picking up the poop."

"Really?" I smile long and hard at Frank. "I just ran off your last girlfriend and now I come bearing puppies and that's cool?"

"*You* didn't run her off. It just fizzled."

"She said she didn't like your roommate. That would be me."

"That was after I made her mad with my utmost honesty," he says, placing his hand over his heart. "I said, 'Look, it's over. We fizzled.' That pissed her off because I beat her to the punch. If I'd waited five minutes she would have dumped my behind."

"Ha!"

Franks laughs before shoveling in a spoonful of ice cream.

"Why are you being so good to me?" I ask.

He shrugs.

"Do you feel sorry for me or something?"

"Come on, we're friends," he says, putting his cap back on. "Speaking of which, how about I make Thanksgiving dinner. My parents aren't coming up this year. I thought I'd cook and we'll invite Rosie and your cousin. I'll ask Mikey and a few friends."

"And the puppies, of course," I say happily.

"We're having the puppies for dessert," he says, sliding his eyes over to me.

"You're terrible!" I cry. I clobber him with a pillow and he clobbers me back. I stand on the couch in my socks and wallop him over the head and then he chases me around the living room. When he pins me, I cry, "You win, you win." But as he lets me go, I slug him one more time, so he pins me again. "Truce," I say.

"Liar," he says, knowing my tricks.

"Really," I say, and when he lets me go I reach for a pillow, but he's too fast for me. "Truce. Honest to god," I say, holding up my hands and catching my breath. He lets me go, and I behave myself.

"Thank you, Frank," I say, sinking down on the couch. "About the dogs, I mean."

"Of course," he says.

"So why are you being so good to me?"

He lifts his bowl to his mouth and slurps down the melted ice cream. "Because I like who I am when I'm being good," he says.

Thanksgiving morning Frank and I start early. He cleans and stuffs the turkey. I make candied yams and peel a whole five-pound bag of potatoes until my hand is sore. All morning and into the afternoon, Frank and I peel and chop and work our butts off. The puppies run around the house, yapping and jumping on each other. They go at it in bursts of energy, and then they conk out in little heaps in the middle of the kitchen floor. "Move it," Frank says, scooting them over to the wall with his slippered foot.

Angie and Rosie come over with pies. "Skate," Rosie says, pulling me into the bathroom, looking wild-eyed. "Perry called a couple times this morning looking for you. He said to meet him on the boardwalk at nine o'clock tonight. By Denardino's." My heart speeds up, and I catch a look at myself in the mirror. I'm flushed and a smile creeps across my face. "You'll go, won't you?" Rosie asks, grabbing my arm. I nod.

By late afternoon everyone is here, and we're tripping over each other in the kitchen. We put the food on the table, make plates for ourselves, and crowd into the living room to eat. Everything is super yummy, and it's a good time. We eat, we yak, we rest, then we go back for seconds.

"Pie?" Angie says as we lounge around the living room like slugs. We have room somehow. I'm glad when Nick shows up and joins us for dessert. As I walk out of the kitchen with a pile of napkins, I see Nick feeding Rosie a bite of sweet potato pie off his fork.

After everyone leaves, Frank and I attack the kitchen. We take turns washing and drying, and it takes forever. Midway through I yell, "Break!" and head for the couch.

"Don't lose steam now, LD. We're almost there." But I ignore him and instantly fall asleep. A little while later I wake with Barney on my chest, licking my neck. "Come on," Frank says, snapping his fingers in my face. "Chop-chop."

"Now?" I say.

"Naturally." So we attack the kitchen again. This time it's the slimy turkey pan and crusted mashed potato pot. Brillo. More Brillo. It's endless. Finally, the dishes are done. I collapse on the living room carpet, splayed like a starfish. Frank staggers to the couch and drops. "Holy freakin-noli!" he cries.

As the clock on the TV hits eight-thirty, I think about not showing up on the boardwalk. I could blow Perry off. I mean, what does he want? He dumped me. He has a new girlfriend. I feed the puppies, and soon they're yawning. They fall asleep as I pet their soft heads and rub their ears. "Sweet boy," I whisper to Barney. "Sweet girl," I say to Lorry.

At five to nine, though, I jump up and put on my coat. Just then the phone rings, and Frank lazily reaches for it. "Hello, you," he says, perking up, a big old smile breaking across his face. Another LD, no doubt.

It's cold and gusty as I ride up to the boardwalk, and Perry is waiting, huddled next to the pier, shivering.

"Hey," he says.

"Hey."

We head into Denardino's and order Cokes and take a booth in the back by the ovens.

"How goes it?" he asks me.

"Pretty good." He looks the same as he's been looking all fall, which means exactly the same—like Perry— but also different. He has a new Phish T-shirt and his hair is the longest it's ever been. He looks so good to me that it's hard to sit across from him.

"You have to come over tomorrow for leftovers. Plus my mom will probably make mac 'n' cheese."

I force a smile but don't say anything. Does he have any idea I was there at that party that night? Does he know who I was with and how much I drank? Does he know what happened in the bathroom? Could he know? But seeing him slouched over his Coke, glancing up and smiling at me now and then, telling me about school and his friends, I'm sure he has no idea. No idea at all. In a weird way, he feels like a stranger to me, even though I know him better than anybody. He talks a lot, rattling on and on.

He tells me Eleanor is his girlfriend. *I know.* He

explains patiently that I met her when I came up that first night. *I know.* He crunches on an ice cube as he tells me things are *pretty good. Pretty good,* he keeps saying. *Pretty good.* He doesn't look at me as he talks. "You know what it is," he says. "She's so *nice.* She's so *thoughtful.* She bought me a pencil sharpener when my pencils got stubby. When I had a cold she bought me those puffy tissues—the ones that don't make your nose all red when you blow like five hundred times. She always does what she says she's going to. She eats five servings of fruits and vegetables every day. She's just so freaking cheerful. All the time. She's exhausting." He shakes his head and takes a big swallow of soda.

"I don't get it," I say.

"I don't either. I totally like her, but I don't know."

"So you're going to break up with her?"

"I don't know. Do you miss me?" he asks, looking right at me.

"No," I lie.

He smiles. "A little bit, Skate?"

"You dumped me, remember? I ran after you in the street. I wanted to tell you about the Old Crow. He broke into the jail pharmacy, downed a bunch of cough syrup, and lost visiting privileges. Got an extra six weeks added onto his sentence. He has to attend AA twice a day now."

"Oh man," Perry says.

"Poor you," I say. "With your puffy tissues and your

nice girlfriend." I take a napkin out of the dispenser and swipe at the water ring from my soda.

Perry's face turns splotchy red. "Dude," he says, blowing out a puff of air. "You are totally right. God, I sound like a jerk."

I shake my head and shrug. I miss the puppies right then. I think about telling Perry about them but I don't want to tell him I live at Frank's, so I don't say anything.

"You know," Perry says, watching as Gino tosses the dough and whirls it around his fists. "Sometimes you're a pain in the butt, Skate. You can be snotty when you're mad. Every now and then I want to wring your neck. But you're real. You're *real*. . . ." He looks at me. "Do you think," he says quietly, "you might miss me some-time soon?"

"Then what?" I say, shredding the wet napkin on my lap.

His eyes soften as he leans across the table toward me. "Then we might do something about it."

"Perry, I have to go." I grab my board and slide out of the booth.

Rosie

Skate walks in the door as I'm trying to decide if I want to go to the meeting. I have one arm in the sleeve of my jacket. I told Gus I might come and tried to tell Nick, but he was weird in school today. Didn't wait for me after geometry and didn't get on the bus with me. Worse, there's the letter. I hand it to Skate. It's from our dad and addressed to *Rosie & Skate Meyers* in spidery handwriting that you might think is a shaky, drunken hand but is just how he writes, even sober. When I got home from school it was sitting in the mailbox. *Open me, open me,* it demands. But I won't. I can't. Now Skate holds it in her hand, unopened. We look at each other, Skate's eyes wide and blue.

"Where are you going?" she asks.

I pull my arm out of the sleeve and sit on the staircase with my jacket bunched on my lap. "Maybe a meeting or maybe not."

"Drama Queen? Hey, I'll go with you," she says, tossing the letter on top of the other mail.

"*You?* Really?"

But she's already out the door, calling "Come on." So I pull on my jacket and wrap a scarf around my neck.

Outside, Skate pushes past me back into the house, returning for the dreaded letter. "Come on. Afterward we'll go to Carolanne's for a hamburger and maybe we'll open this sucker."

Nick is already there, munching on a cookie. He looks surprised to see me and gives me a lame wave. The wave isn't inviting enough to plop down next to him, so I linger, deciding I'll sit next to him only if he looks up at me in the next thirty seconds. His eyes meet mine on the count of twelve, but then for some reason I no longer want to sit next to him. But it seems rude not to, so I slide into a chair and we smile, but neither of us says anything. I'm glad when Skate comes over, board in one hand, Cherry Coke in the other, and one of Gus's cookies sticking out of her mouth. "Hey, Nick," she says, settling into a chair.

"Hey, Skate," he says. "Didn't expect to see you here."

"Weird, I know," she says coolly. "I came for the cookies." She gets up and grabs a handful from the foil-lined shoe box to share with us. So we all chew and don't talk. A couple days ago I asked her if she met up with Perry on the boardwalk, like he wanted her to. "Don't ask," she said, looking away. So I shut up and waited for her to change her mind. She didn't. What a threesome we are. Gus saves us by pulling up a chair and sitting on it backward. He makes small talk until the meeting starts.

Nick gives an update on his dad. He's drinking, but not getting smashed. That's the good news. The bad news is that he's moodier. "When he's in a mood he always picks a fight with me," Nick says.

"And do you let him?" Gus asks.

"Yeah, I guess," Nick says, sinking low in his chair.

"Why not walk away?"

"Easy to say," Nick says. "When he's in a mood, he picks a fight and always winds up pissing me off."

"Look," Gus says, "if you always do what you've always done, you'll always get what you always got."

Skate snorts in my ear, and I shoot her a look. "Relax. I *like* it," she whispers. But later in the meeting when Gus says, "You have to have a higher spirit. You have to believe in something bigger than yourself," she gives me a deliciously obnoxious eye roll.

Afterward as I'm unlocking my bike, Nick comes up. "Did you do the geometry homework?"

"Not yet," I say.

"Want me to come over and we'll do it?"

"I would, definitely," I say. "But I'm hanging out with Skate—"

"No worries," he says, backing away.

"Later?" I blurt out.

"How later?"

"Later later," I say. Nick shrugs and turns.

"Well," Skate says, sliding into a booth at the diner. "Drama Queen is still not my thing."

"Why'd you want to go?"

"I guess I just . . . Oh, I don't know. Don't pain my butt, Rosie."

"*Touchy*," I say.

She shrugs and flips her hair off her shoulders and studies the menu for a second. "Cheeseburger," she says, slapping it shut. She pulls out the letter, slits it open, reads it, then hands it over to me.

> *Dear girls,*
>
> > *My Rosie and Skate,*
> > *Lights in the dark,*
> > *Do you think you might find a way to believe in me? Truth is, I don't know if I believe in me. But maybe if I know you're there in the house, thinking of me a little, I'll find a way to live without a drink.*
> > *Scratch that. I can't ask that. I'll believe in me. Can you believe in that?*
>
> > > > *With love,*
> > > > *your Dad*

We're staring at each other when the waitress comes over with her pad. So we order two cheeseburgers, extra pickles, and one order of fries. Skate reads the letter again, and then I do.

"He thinks you live in the house," I say.

"Yeah, I guess he would."

"I wish you and the puppies were coming home . . . like we planned."

"You can come visit anytime," she says.

"That's not what I mean. I wish you would come home."

"I don't know where home is."

Aren't I a part of home? I want to say.

It doesn't take long for our order to arrive, and as soon as Skate's plate hits the table, she lifts her burger and bites into it.

I finger the edge of the letter. "Never in a million years could he have expected this is where he'd end up." I picture his orange jumpsuit, the gray visitors' room, the slice of sky through the smudged window, the cement sitting area in the yard, his little locker. "Nobody thinks they'll sink so low."

"Nope." Skate takes a juicy bite of pickle.

"But it happens."

"Yep."

"Say something," I say.

"Rosie," she says, popping the rest of the pickle into her mouth and chewing furiously. "It's not going to happen to us."

"I know that."

"No, you don't. I can tell. Repeat after me: It's never going to happen to us. Here, eat." She pushes the plate of French fries toward me, and I douse them with ketchup.

"Of course it's not going to happen to us. Geez, Skate."

"Don't geez me. You're the one who's worrying."

"I just don't get it. I never have. I can't understand him. What he does . . . who he is . . ." I shake my head. "I don't get it."

"Nobody gets it. *He* doesn't get it. So don't knock yourself out. How's things with Nick, anyway?" she asks. "At Drama Queen the two of you looked like somebody died, if you want to know the truth."

"Sometimes I look at Nick and think *yes!* And sometimes I just . . ."

"Just what?"

"I don't know . . . ," I say. "Do you think there's something wrong with me, Skate?"

"Relax, will you?" She pops a fry into her mouth.

"You and Perry never ran hot and cold."

"We were smokin' hot till he went to college," she says, and a secret little smile spreads across her face.

"Great. Thanks."

"Look, maybe Nick isn't exactly right for you. Like how if you're a size seven shoe, a six and a half might fit too, but it pinches after a while. Maybe he's a six and a half on your seven foot. You know?"

"But when it's good, it's good."

"What do I know, Rosie? I've been dumped." She makes a face at her hamburger and lets it drop to the plate in a greasy splat.

"Perry'll come around. He wanted to see you, right?"

"He doesn't know what he wants."

But I think he does. When he called the house on Thanksgiving morning, looking for Skate and wanting to meet her on the boardwalk, I could hear him missing her. I heard it in his voice.

Once last summer—early summer, when the days are really long—they'd been surfing late in the day and carried their boards back to our shed. I was in the outside shower rinsing off my raft. They didn't see me and for some reason I didn't let on I was there. Through a slit in the door I watched Perry stack the boards, and then he turned to Skate and smiled at her. He gathered up the wet hair that clung to her back and squeezed the water out it, the drops hitting the stones. Then he kissed her lips like she was a tender thing. "What a girl you are," he whispered, and I swooned there in the shower, clutching my raft, my eyes pricking. Would I ever know that?

"Are you gonna go to college?" I ask, forking up some cole slaw.

"Yeah, I guess. Hey, did I tell you I did pretty good on the PSAT?"

"What do you want to do, Skate?"

"When I grow up?" she says, teasing me. "No clue. Something."

"I might be a physician's assistant."

"Why not a doctor? Geez." She licks ketchup from her lip.

"I don't think I want to go to school that long, and besides, a physician's assistant can do a lot of what a doctor does—examine you and write prescriptions." Last year when I had a wicked sore throat I was treated by a physician's assistant at the clinic. She was young and nice and took a throat culture. She had me feeling better even before the antibiotics kicked in. I eat a few ketchup-smothered fries and look at the gloomy white envelope with the spidery handwriting sitting there on the table. "Oh, I'm so tired of him."

"I've been tired of him for years." Skate wipes her greasy hands on a napkin. "But when he gets his visiting privileges back I'm gonna visit."

"You are not!"

"I am."

"Don't tell me you're giving him a break!"

"Oh, I'm not giving the Old Crow a break," Skate says. "Trust me."

"So why go?"

"Can't a person say hello?"

"When did you decide?"

"Right now." Skate balls up her napkin. "How does that thing go? 'If you always do what you've always done, you'll always get what you always got.' Maybe I'm switching things up."

I stare at the letter, then at my sister. "Well, I'm not going." Maybe I've switched it up too.

"Funny, isn't it?" Skate says, pocketing the letter.

Back at home, the phone rings as I walk in. "Hello," I say, hoping maybe it's Nick and that he's the right size after all.

"Rosie, is she there?" Perry asks.

"Perry, hi!" I blurt out. "She's not, but I'll be sure to tell her to call you." Oh, how much I want to tell him I think they belong together, that he just needs to give Skate some time . . . but something stops me. I hang up and sink into a kitchen chair, wondering if I should have said it. The phone rings again, and I'm sure it's Perry, so I lunge for it.

"Hi, is Angie around?" a girl asks.

"Sure," I say, surprised. Angie doesn't get a lot of calls. I yell up to her, and as I turn, Nick is looking in the kitchen window at me. "Hey," I say, letting him in.

"Hey, guys," Angie says as she flies past us and picks up the phone. "I'm so glad you called back," she says, laughing. "It's so great to hear your voice."

"Is it too late?" Nick whispers shyly.

"No, no, let's do the geometry. Let's go up."

So for the next forty-five minutes we spread out on my floor and do the problems. Afterward, Nick says, "I guess I should go." I don't want him to yet, but I wonder what he'll think I mean if I say that. Nick must be thinking the same thing, 'cause he sits there and doesn't move.

"You could stay for a little bit," I say, fiddling with the radio.

"All right," he says. "We could just kiss. If you feel like it."

"I feel like it," I say.

"Okay then." He hooks his hair behind his ears, which are flaming pink, and this makes me smile and feel less afraid. Not that I'm frightened or anything.

"Ready when you are," he tries to say with a straight face, but he laughs.

"Come and get me," I say, and blush.

"Here I come," he says, his face bright and happy. I giggle, and he scoots across the floor, wearing a little smile that makes me feel fluttery. And he kisses me a few times. "You taste like ketchup."

"Oh, gross." I start to get up.

"Nah, it's all right," he says, pulling me back down. So we kiss for a while until the floor feels too hard.

"Can we lie down?" he asks.

"Okay." I turn down the radio and dim the light and we crawl under the quilt. With the light low, I feel braver. "Nick, why is it sometimes hard between us?"

"I don't know."

"I don't know either," I say.

"Should we know?"

"Good question." The wind roars at the window, rattling the pane. I slide closer to him and feel his warmth under the quilt. There are many things I don't know, but even so, I'm just happy he's here with me now.

"Can we get back to the kissing?" he says, nuzzling me.

I nod, and that's all we do. Kiss. It's very nice, and we must grow sleepy. The next thing I know the sun is streaming in. Nick wakes next to me.

"Crap," he says, popping out of bed. He gathers his stuff, squeezes my hand, and tells me he'll see me in homeroom.

Skate

Rosie tells me Perry keeps leaving messages at the house. He even called the arcade when I was there, but I shook my head when Frank held out the phone to me. Frank unapologetically told him, "Sorry, dude. Not here," and hung up. I haven't told Frank what happened, that Perry wants me back.

After school, I take the bus to Little Mermaid and go to the house. I take the phone into my room and sit on the bed. The easiest thing in the world would be to say *yes*. I call Perry, hoping it goes to voice mail, but he picks up on the first ring.

"Finally," he says.

"Stop calling me so much."

"Well, finally," he says again.

He's outside. I hear voices and traffic.

"Where are you right now?"

"I'm running around like a madman. I just picked up my paycheck and I'm headed to the ATM, then I'm off

to the history department to drop off a late paper. Then
I'm returning some books to the library. What are you
doing?"

"I'll go to the arcade and work a couple hours."

"I wish I could beam you into the cafeteria later.
They're having meatballs and sausage tonight."

"Mmm . . . So why's your paper late?" I ask.

"Oh, I was dillydallying."

"Hey, Perry, I was thinking today . . . Do you remember that first time in the tub?"

"I sure do," he says, his voice sweet and low.

Perry and I had only known each other a few weeks
when Hal, Julia's boyfriend, had a party at his place, and
Perry invited me along. We hung outside on the porch
glider wrapped in a blanket. As the party grew noisy
Perry took me on a tour of Hal's big old house on the
bay. On the third floor there was a big bathroom with a
big claw-foot tub, like we have, but much swankier.
Everyone was on the first floor, drinking and mingling,
and we were up there all alone. I turned on the faucets
in the tub. "Let's take a bath."

"Here? Now?"

"Why not?"

"I'm game," Perry said, blushing. So as the room
grew steamy, we took off our clothes in front of each
other, one piece at a time, as if daring each other to
go on.

"Whee!" I said, buck naked.

"Woo-hoo!" Perry said, stepping out of his underpants and kicking them to the wall.

At first we looked into each other's eyes, feeling all giddy, but then we had ourselves a look—a nice long look. A nice long amazing look. I climbed over the edge of the tub a little jittery and sat myself down in the hot water and Perry sank down next to me, twining his long legs with mine.

"That's a nice thing to think about," Perry says.

"Yeah" is all I can say, because remembering is like an ache, but why should it ache, a good memory like that? Maybe it's that Perry is always with me even when he isn't, like now, as he walks down a street in New Brunswick to the ATM. I never have a moment away from him. . . . Funny, since I'm never *with* him either. "You're still with your girlfriend?"

"Yeah, but it's like I told you . . . just say the word, Skate."

"I'm thinking about everything. Don't bug me. I'm thinking. And since when do you say *dillydally*?"

"I don't know." He laughs.

"I gotta go." I hang up the phone and wait for it to start ringing. But it doesn't, and I'm glad.

I ride past the boardwalk, deciding not to work this afternoon. I don't feel like talking. I have a paper to write, and I don't want to do that either, but it's due tomorrow. Guess I'm *dillydallying.* I let myself into Frank's house, and the puppies run up to me, jumping and going crazy because they only have the run of the kitchen when we're not there. I take them into the yard and they go crazy, doing laps. I sit in the rowboat and try to think. The bottom line, it seems to me, is that even though Perry ended it with me and started up with her, I'm the one he wants. Me. But this doesn't thrill me as much as it should. I wonder why. And my unwritten English paper is pissing me off. "Come on, puppies," I say, opening the kitchen door. But they ignore me. So I have to chase and catch them one at a time to get them in the house. And while I sink into the couch with my notebook, Lorry takes a dump on the kitchen floor. "Oh, man, you were just outside!" I yell. I mean to pick it up, but I don't.

Later, when it's dark, Frank comes home. "Oh, crap!" he yells. "Barney, what did you do?"

"Why do you assume it was Barney?" I sit with my notebook and a copy of *Great Expectations,* trying to write my paper.

"He's got a guilty look in his eye. It was you, wasn't it?" he says, bending down to Barney.

"Unbelievable, Frank. You even flirt with girl dogs. For your information, Lorry took that dump."

"Lorry," he says, looking at her sternly. But she looks

up at Frank with big soulful eyes and wags her tail. "Is Skate lying?" he asks her, bending down to pet her. "Was it really you?" he whispers. Barney gets bored and wanders over to me.

"It was your girl, dude," I say. "Leave Barney out of it." He jumps up on the couch and licks my hand.

"So you mean to tell me you watched her take a crap and you left it on my kitchen floor."

"I was planning on picking it up after I finish this paragraph."

"Likely story, Lorry. Well, here you go," he says, handing me a wad of paper towels.

I clean it up, then heave myself back onto the couch and stare at the same half-written paragraph. I like English. I'm good in English. But I can't get past these few sentences.

Frank heads into the kitchen and opens the refrigerator. I hear him unloading grocery bags. "How come you didn't come to work today? I wanted you to order me some new fortunes. I have this catalog. We got to get something better, don't you think? They should be upbeat and funny, maybe. Mine today was *Troubles are to be expected*. Who wants *that*?"

I erase a sentence, waiting for inspiration.

"LD," Frank says, standing over me at the couch.

"Are you talking to me?"

"Naturally," he says.

"What'd you say?"

"Ai-yi-yi." He flings his fortune at me. *Troubles are to be expected.*

I fling it back at him.

"You hungry?" he asks.

I nod.

"I'm gonna make pesto. You want to make a salad?"

"Okay." But I sit there, so Frank raps on my skull.

"Yoohoo," he says. "What's wrong? Why didn't you come to work this afternoon?"

"Sorry."

Frank picks up Lorry and lets her lick his face. "She's in a mood, this one," he tells the puppy. "She sure is."

"Knock it off."

He flops his head back in frustration and heads into the kitchen. I heave myself off the couch and wash lettuce, scrape a carrot, chop a tomato, sprinkle some croutons on top, and set our places.

Then we sit, and Frank rubs his hands together. "De-lish," he says, eyeing his dinner. "So I was saying to you," he says, chewing. "I want you to flip through the catalog and find better fortunes. No *Troubles are to be expected* crap."

"Frank," I yell, "don't be some happy moron. Everyone's got troubles."

He holds his fork in midair. "Do you think everyone wants to pay fifty cents to hear it?"

I try to smile because I know I'm being bitchy. "So what do you want? *Good things are right around the corner! You will travel to many distant lands!*"

"Kind of. Yeah. But maybe a little funnier, you know."

I glare at him, and he smiles down at his spaghetti. "I thought it would be fun. Obviously not."

"I'll find some you funny fortunes, Frank," I say, twirling my spaghetti against my spoon, like he taught me. "No worries."

"Did I do something wrong?" he asks, putting down his fork and looking me in the eye. He needs to shave. His face is stubbly, and he needs a haircut too. His hair flips up every which way as he sits there, watching me, really wanting to know.

"No . . . I'm in a mood. . . . Don't make me tell you."

"Perry?"

I nod.

"So tell me."

"He misses me. . . . He wants . . ."

Frank forks up a big mouthful and chews slowly. "You told him no, I hope."

I shake my head.

"Think about how he was stringing you along. Think about how he kept bailing on you."

"You don't even really know him."

"I know what I know. You want a boyfriend who's never around? Who—"

"It's really none of your business, Frank."

Well, that's a conversation stopper. We finish our dinner without saying a word. He gets up and takes his plate to the sink, and I watch him finger a few strands of spaghetti out of the pot and tilt his head back and drop them in. Neither of us has eaten our salad, but I clean up anyway. I put the leftover spaghetti in a Tupperware bowl, and I wash the pot and the blender. I leave our salads on the counter and flip off the light.

Frank is sitting in the recliner reading the *Asbury Park Press* when I go back to the couch and my notebook. "I made it your business, like it or not," I say. "That wasn't fair. Sorry."

He looks at me over the top of the paper. "Well, what do *I* know? I'm just a happy moron." But he smiles as he says it.

"You're a happy dude, true, but definitely not a moron."

"Why, thank you, LD," he says, giving the newspaper a shake.

I slide down to the floor, where Barney chews on an old slipper. Lorry comes over and yawns puppy breath in my face. "I don't know what to do."

"So he broke up with that girl?"

"Not yet."

"Ha! He hasn't dumped her in case you say no. Now he's stringing *her* along. Ha!"

"Frank!" I say, exasperated. "*You've* strung girls along. *You've* bailed on girlfriends."

"I wouldn't do it to you."

"Why not?"

He lifts the paper back up.

"I love him," I say. "I mean, I loved him. I mean, I don't know anymore."

Frank doesn't say anything, and I try again with my essay.

A little later, Frank wanders into the kitchen and I hear him shaking the salad dressing before he drowns his salad. He always does that, drowns his salad. He stands at the counter crunching and then pads back into the living room and sits on the arm of the couch. "LD," he says, still chewing. "You make me responsible. I never feel that way with a girl. But with you I do. That's why I'd never string you along or bail on you. You're a little bit young for me, true. But . . ." He looks me in the eyes. "I like everything about you."

"Frank," I say, surprised.

"You ever think of me that way?"

"Frank!" I gather up my stuff, shove it all into my backpack.

"What are you doing?"

"I don't know!"

He takes my backpack out of my hands. "Hold it, LD. Hold it right there. Just keep your pants on. We're good together, yeah?"

My eyes sting. "Knock it off!"

"Knock it off?" he asks, looking at me like I'm nuts.

"What are you doing? Just stop!"

"All right. All right." He makes me sit beside him. "Just think about it." He waves his hand in the air. "Just write your paper, and go to school, and order me some new fortunes. But sleep on it. Okay? I'm not going anywhere."

As I put on my jacket, the puppies look up at me hopefully, thinking maybe I'm taking them outside. "Look, I have to write this wicked paper and I can't do it here. I'm going to the house and taking Barney with me, okay?" I put an old towel in my backpack and stick the puppy inside so just his head peers out. He squirms all around, not liking it one bit.

Frank watches me unhappily from the doorway as I wrap the backpack around the front of me and get on my board. It's a cold night. "Here we go," I whisper down to Barney. Barney likes it, though, and stops squirming once we get moving. His little ears flop back in the wind. Oh, what has Frank gone and done?

I start spending more and more time at my house. Rosie and Angie are crazy about Barney, and it is sort of nice to be back in my own room, my own bed, under my own quilt with my own window overlooking the ocean. At first I alternated puppies, 'cause I miss Lorry too, but I couldn't separate Frank from his love for too long. So it's mostly Barney I take. I order Frank some funny fortunes that I know he'll like. I work when I say I will. I go to school. I even sleep on Frank's couch once in a while.

We have this thing called Frank's Two Minutes, where he makes a pitch about why we should be together. He'll say, "Give me two minutes, LD." Then he'll launch into stuff like "We both like to eat." And I'll say, "Well, doesn't everybody?" and he'll say, "Some of us like to more than others." Or he'll say, "We both like late-night reruns, we both like the arcade, we both like to surf." Usually we wind up laughing. I'm not worried about hurting Frank's feelings. For now this idea has grabbed hold of him, but he's mostly an easy person, and I don't see him staying stuck on it. Besides, he has plenty of other LDs calling, and he talks to them happily enough.

But sometimes I look at Frank and I think, Yeah, why not? Mostly, though, I think about Perry. Perry crowds my head and my dreams. Some mornings I wake sweaty and weak. But I don't make up my mind about him. I don't call him either. I just try the best I can to get through my days. After school there's Barney or work. There's homework. There's hanging out with Rosie. There's Rosie with Nick, there's Rosie and Angie. There's French fries at Carolanne's. There's dinner at Frank's some nights.

This is how it goes as we head into Christmas. Angie lugs home a Charlie Brown tree, and Rosie and I tease her nonstop until she carts it off to her room with a huff.

Then the three of us get a real tree. Rosie, who has the patience of a saint, strings popcorn, one little piece at a time. I dig up boxes of ornaments from the junk room and hang the colored balls on the branches.

And then the Old Crow has visiting privileges again. I ask Angie to take me, but she's working a lot at the salon now. She offers to switch her schedule but I say no. Julia would take me. I know that. But I ask Frank, who says of course. So we drive out one cold, sunny afternoon.

The first thing is he looks good. Best he's looked in years. Who would think he'd bloom in the Ocean Grove Correctional Facility, like some crazy jail flower? I plunk myself down across from him and introduce Frank. After they say hello, Frank skedaddles to another table with a newspaper.

"Didn't think I'd see you," my dad says, breaking into a smile.

"Well, here I am."

"Wonderful," he says. "No Rosie?"

"Nope. No Rosie."

"Ah, well . . . It's good to see you, Skate."

"First, let me get this off my chest," I say, staring him down. "Don't make any promises."

"Okay," he says simply.

"Really?" I say, wriggling out of my jacket. "Cool."

Then he has a million questions. How am I? How's school? What am I doing with myself?

"And how's your boyfriend?" he asks.

"We ended it."

The Old Crow smiles sadly at me. "His loss."

"Mine too. Do you remember Perry?"

"The black-haired boy. Good-looking fellow."

I nod. "He's at Rutgers. Started this year. Just too hard on both of us."

"There's plenty of fish in the sea, kid."

"But who wants to go out with a fish?" It comes to me then that if I'm talking about Perry as if it's really over, then maybe it is.

"Get yourself a tuna or a mackerel, but stay away from the bottom-feeders." My dad jerks his thumb toward Frank. "And this guy?"

"Oh, he's my boss at Lucky Louie's. He's Louie's son. Louie spends all his time in Florida now except for the summer. Frank runs the show in the off-seasons."

My dad nods.

"He's a nice guy," I say, looking over at Frank. "He makes his own ravioli."

"That guy *there*?" my dad teases.

"Right *there*." I tease back. "The Mermaid Heights ravioli man."

"And you cook?"

"No, but I sure like to eat, so I better get crackin', huh?"

"I thought of you just yesterday, Skate. You were

always the one with the peanut butter and jelly. What a sticky mess you'd make."

"I haven't had a peanut butter and jelly sandwich in ages," I say, getting hungry.

"Well, I had one yesterday."

"You did not."

"Swear it," he says, lifting his hand. "It's the basics when you're in the slammer. It wasn't bad either." He looks down at the table for a minute, then up at me. "Why no Rosie today?"

"Honestly, Dad, I think she's had it with you."

"Oh dear," he says.

"I'm not going to sugarcoat it," I say. "We've both really had it up to here."

He nods.

"It had to be said. Sorry," I say. For being blunt, but not for saying it.

He nods again and half smiles and lowers his eyes.

"This is going to sound weird," I say, leaning toward him. "But will you tell me something about Mom? I know all the stories. I've seen all the pictures. Tell me something I *don't* know."

"Let me see . . . something you don't know . . . She had no sense of direction. Could get lost driving to the grocery store."

"Yeah, okay. But can't you do a little better than that?"

"How about I think about it and get back to you."

"Okay. That works."

"You're thinking about her?" he asks.

"I guess so. Well," I say, reaching for my jacket. "I just wanted to say hello and all."

"Hello and all," he says, and smiles. "I'm glad, honey. I'm glad."

Rosie

It's so good to have Skate back in the house! We sit on the floor in her room wrapping presents in paper decorated with Santas ice-fishing on a pond. Skate wraps and I'm on ribbon duty, while Barney noses into everything.

We bought Angie a bathing suit. She says she's going to fit into a size 8 by summer if it kills her. So we bought her a size 8 for inspiration, a shiny little purple number with beaded straps. Half-price on the boardwalk! We also got her sparkly eye shadow, lip gloss, nail polish, and jeweled barrettes at the drugstore. She officially ended things with her boyfriend—they had a long talk on the phone one night.

"Oh, guess what I got Gus!" I say, springing to my feet.

"A sense of humor," Skate says, ripping off a piece of tape. I swat her on the head with the roll of wrapping paper. "Kidding," she says with a smirk.

At the rummage sale at St. Joseph By the Sea I found

some old-fashioned cookie cutters—a flounder, a flip-flop, and a crab. "A quarter each. Seventy-five cents!"

"Cool," Skate says, fingering them. "His cookies are good. I'll give him that."

For Skate, I found a near-perfect light blue cashmere turtleneck. It has only the tiniest moth hole and Angie said she can fix it, but Skate kind of likes the holes.

"Know what I'm doing for Frank?" she says. "I ordered new cards for the fortune-telling machine at the arcade, and I picked out the best ones. On Christmas Eve when he's having dinner with his parents I'll go over to his house and hide them—in his toaster oven, silverware drawer, laundry basket, medicine cabinet, his Cocoa Puffs." She shows me the stack and I flip through them: *I'm happy to report you will be filthy rich! I see many friends and a room filled with laughter—check your zipper. An open mind is fine as long as your brains don't fall out. You'll get everything you want and then some!*

"I love them!" I cry.

"Here's a good one for the Old Crow," she says, pulling out a card. *"Try something different—you and everyone you know will be pleased."*

"Not to mention shocked."

Skate laughs. "Speaking of the Old Crow, did I tell you he looks good?"

"How *good*?"

"You know, good. Not dazed or droopy or sad. *Good.*" Skate takes the scissors from me and recurls the ribbon I just curled and then admires her work. So bossy she is. "Just go say Merry Christmas, Rosie. Just go for a little while."

"I can't bear him," I say.

"Join the club," she says. "But listen. Go say Merry Christmas, and then give him a piece of your mind."

I lie down on the floor and let Barney jump on me. I think about the last times I saw my dad, how small and shrunken he looked, as if his skin were too big for him. "Oh, I can't do that."

"Of course you can." Skate gives me a kick. "It's time. It's about damn time."

I let out a long sigh. Barney cocks his head and barks.

"Cheer up, I have something for you," Skate says. "I was going to put these in your stocking, but you can have them now." She takes another stack of fortunes out of her nightstand. "Handpicked just for you. A month's supply." I flip through them. *You got it going on! Yes, yes, yes! I see money, honey! When in doubt you always choose well!*

"I love them!" I cry. "I love all the exclamation points!"

It's time. It's about damn time. All week those words follow me down the halls at school and echo in my head on the bus and whisper to me late at night under the covers. Should I visit my dad? I take a fortune from the stack one morning and it reads: *Being wimpy makes you shrimpy—stand tall!* I call Nick to ask his opinion, but once I have him on the phone I can't get myself to talk about it. So instead I ask him over to do homework, but he says he has a load of laundry to do, if he's going to have clean socks for the morning, plus maybe he's coming down with something because he feels sort of headachy, and then we're back in the weird place, because I'm sure he just doesn't want to come over. I mean, *socks*! And everything feels worse, much worse. But when the weekend rolls around I find myself asking Angie if she'll take me to the jail before she goes to the salon.

I don't want to watch him walk across the room in his orange jumpsuit. I can't bear that, so I go to the restroom and hang out in the stall with the leaky faucet and the words *this sucks weenies* carved into the wall until I'm sure he's already seated in the ugly gray room. When I finally poke my head in, there he is next to Angie.

"Hey," I say, sliding in across from him. Angie pats his shoulder and moves off to another table.

"Hi, honey." He reaches across the table and squeezes my hand. I let him, for a second, but then I put my hands in my lap. Skate was right. He does look pretty good. His eyes are brightly blue, like always, and fixed right on me. He's not far away, as he sometimes is. He's not as bony either. "I'm glad you came."

"Will you, you know, celebrate in here?" I ask. Someone has hung a Frosty the Snowman cutout in the window.

"Not much. It doesn't matter, love. I'll go to a meeting. I work in the kitchen too. I like cooking." He moves his hand like he's shaking a frying pan. "It's something to do."

I nod. "You get out in a couple of months," I say.

"Yes, ma'am," he says, sitting up straighter, as if he's ready to spring out of this place.

"I can't keep worrying about you."

"I don't want you to, honey. Let me worry about me."

I nod.

"Well," he says, smoothing his sleeve. "It's one day at a time." He sits there looking pleased with himself, and it makes me angry. "Tell me about school and everything."

"There's not much to tell, really."

"Come on," he says.

"Why don't you tell me something?" I say.

"I'm reading a book written by the Dalai Lama. Quite a guy, that one." And he starts to tell me why the Dalai Lama is quite a guy, but I can barely listen. I pull on a hangnail and then bite it with my teeth. I tune in to hear him say, "I've been thinking about when I get home. Getting a job. My sponsor is helping me with that. Oh, I want to come home, Rosie. It's a countdown. When I wake up—" He makes an X in the air. "I cross out another day that's over in here. Soon, soon," he says.

"Well," I say.

"Do you . . ." He tilts his head to the side. "Do you want me to come home?"

"I don't know," I mumble.

His eyes meet mine and he gives me one of those weary, honest smiles that says *Yup, I sure have screwed up.* I would like to forgive him then. But in the next second he clears his throat and says, "I guess all we can do is take it one day at a time."

"I hate that!" I say loud enough that a few heads turn. "I hate that. You make it sound easy. 'One day at a time'! Well, screw it."

"Rosie—"

"What about all the *days* you broke your promises? What about the *day* you took money—my money—out of my sock drawer? It was mine, Dad. And you took it. You screw up time after time. . . ." I can't even look at him. "I'm so sick of it," I whisper, heating up all over again.

"I—"

"You what? You what? Listen, you *look* good right now. You *sound* good. I see you believe it's all gonna work out. . . . But what about a week after you get home? What about three days after you get home? What about an hour after you get home? I can see it." I close my eyes, picturing him on the sunporch gurgling away, talking to himself, clutching his bottle of Old Crow. "If you start up again, I'll feel stunned. Like I always do. How many times can a person be stunned? How many?" I look around the room wildly and then turn away from him.

We don't say anything for a while. From the corner of my eye, I see his hand hover over mine, but it doesn't land. "What can I do, love?" he finally says.

"I can't be your believer. Don't try to make me believe. I won't be disappointed." The words are rushing out by themselves and I feel myself burn with heat, a deep burn.

"You don't have to believe. I can handle you not believing." And I can see that maybe he can, and in a funny way it makes me kind of mad.

"When you get home, I'll be friendly and everything," I say quietly. "But believing is not my job. And if you . . . if you . . . Don't make me think that if only I believed it wouldn't have happened. . . ."

"I won't blame you," he says, lowering his eyes.

I start to calm down and concentrate on my hangnail. A pearl of blood wells near the torn skin.

"I'll pay you back," he says.

"It was three hundred dollars," I remind him.

"I have to start working first. Which means getting a job. But I'll pay you back."

I nod.

I stare at the smudged window with the smiling top-hatted Frosty. "Dad, do you think you're never ever ever gonna . . ." I say it like it can't possibly be true. Like the sun will never shine again or the earth won't turn.

"Well, honey," he says. "That's what I'm trying for."

"Good luck," I say, and it comes out kind of snotty,

like *Yeah right,* but that's not what I mean at all. What I mean is *Please just do it this time.*

He lets out a sigh that deflates him a little. "I don't know why, Rosie girl. I've never known why." He shakes his head and spurts out a little laugh. "I'm trying to make this time different. But words don't mean anything. It's not the words. . . . All the sorrys in the world mean diddly-squat."

I nod. There are no right words, definitely no magic words, no words that can fix everything. So we sit together without saying anything much. Outside, fat snowflakes fall from the sky. We watch them melt against the pane.

"Merry Christmas," I finally say.

"To you too, love."

"I'm exhausted." I rub my hands over my face. "I need a nap. I'm gonna go, okay?"

He nods. I quickly kiss his cheek and then rush out of there with Angie following me.

Angie asks if I want to take a walk on the beach before she goes to the salon—she's really into walking these days—but I'm tired, just wiped out. "Come on," she says, slinging an arm around me. "It'll wake you up." She puts Barney on a leash, but he finds it insulting. He keeps turning and giving it a long look, then attacking it. Angie tries to reason with him. "I don't want you running away, buddy boy." And they're off, but I can barely keep up. It's a bright cold day, the sun now shining high in the sky.

The flurries have stopped. Christmas Eve is tomorrow. Presents have been wrapped and the stockings have been hung, even two little ones for Barney and Lorry, who are getting chew toys. Then there's New Year's. The end of the old, beginning of the new. But what's in store?

I squint up at the sun, shielding my eyes, and watch Angie and Barney get farther away from me. I blink at the waves, barely able to keep awake. I feel sort of drugged, so wickedly tired. I was going to make fudge this afternoon—my Christmas present to Nick. But later. It will have to be later. I drag myself along the dunes back to the house, upstairs to my room, where I push off my sneakers and fall onto the bed. And I sleep for a long time.

"Rosie," I hear. "Rosie." Nick pokes his head through my bedroom door, letting in a sliver of light. "Are you all right?" A wet nose nudges my hand, and I pet Barney's head. It's dark out and the half-full moon is visible out the window.

"Nick!" I say, sitting up, feeling so rested.

He comes in and flips on the light. I squint. "Are you all right? I came over before and Skate said you crashed. And here you are still under the covers. . . ."

"Let's go outside," I say, bouncing out of bed. "Wait here." I go to the bathroom and brush my teeth and comb my hair and put on a coat of Maybelline Great Lash. I dash back into my room and plop on the floor, working my feet into my sneakers.

"What's with you?" Nick asks.

"Come on." I fly down the stairs with Barney at my heels.

"It's freezing out," Nick calls.

I grab my jacket and scarf and run out to the beach, where the whipping wind roars. I run across the sand with Barney chasing me. The sky is hugely dark, and I tilt my head back and gulp it in. Nick stands on the sand with his hands pushed into his pockets, jumping from foot to foot. "Rosie, I'm freezing my butt off."

"Then run," I tell him as I whiz past. He joins me and we make a big loop with old Barney barking and leaping and attacking our legs.

Nick grabs me finally. "Whoa, girl," he says. "Why you so wound up?"

"I don't know!" I say. I pull my hood up, jump up and down a few times, and then run like mad down to the water's edge, where the wet sand gives a little and slows me down. Then I hightail it up to the dunes as fast as I can go and collapse on the sand. Barney, totally nuts now, leaps on top of me, ears up, tail wagging. Nick jogs over and drops down next to us.

"I told him off!" I shout above the wind.

"Barney?"

I laugh. "I went to the jail today."

Nick smiles slowly. "You told him off? Tell me."

I flop back on my elbows and think about that. "I'm not sure I can explain."

"Try," Nick whispers, curling against me, away from the wind.

"I got pissed," I say. "Really pissed off." I make my eyes wide and Nick mimics me.

"You, who never gets mad at him . . ."

"Me," I agree.

"So, good."

Above us the winter sky is dark and filled with thin webby clouds. And down here we shiver together on the dune, our teeth chattering, while Barney chews happily on Nick's sleeve.

"You know, my old man is still semi-sober these days," Nick says. "Good, huh? But what a crab-ass he is."

"Steer clear."

"You said it." He rolls his eyes. "You know what I'm about ready to do? I'm about ready to go to the freaking liquor store and buy him a bottle of vodka. 'Here,' I'll say. 'Cheers.' "

"Ha!" I laugh.

"And what did your dad say?" Nick says. "When you told him off?"

"He listened. He listened to me."

"I got to hand it to you, Rosie," Nick says, clapping me on the back. "I'm proud."

"Why, thank you, Nicholas." I feel a smile spread across my face. "Come on," I say, jumping up. I look to the house, where our lit-up Christmas tree glimmers and winks in the window. "Let's warm up."

Skate

It's New Year's Eve and my birthday eve. I was a New Year's Day baby, the first born in Ocean County seventeen years ago at 6:00 a.m. on the start of the New Year.

I ride over to Julia's because she's made me a chocolate layer cake. Tomorrow she has plans with Hal, and tonight everybody has plans, and I'm working this afternoon. So a cake breakfast it is.

The lagoon has a layer of ice, and I shiver as I hurry to the door. Julia is putting finishing touches on the icing. She hugs me. "Happy birthday, Skate."

I squeeze her back and slide into a chair. "No Perry?"

"He's in and out. It turns out a couple of his friends live across the bay." She licks a finger and studies the cake. She's even made a skateboard out of a wafer and mini chocolate morsels.

Julia pours me a glass of milk and herself a cup of coffee. "Ta-da," she says, putting the lit-up cake in front of me.

"You're not going to sing, I hope?" I joke.

"I'll spare you."

I blow out the candles. To be happy again. That's my wish.

"You look better, Skate," Julia says as we chow down. "You have your spark back."

"Oh yeah? What's my spark like?"

"Sparkly." She smiles, showing her teeth.

"You can do better than that."

"You look pretty good, kiddo."

I smile into my cake and take a big bite. "Yum," I say with my mouth full—so creamy and chocolaty.

Perry's backpack sits by the front door, half-open, spilling out books, clothes, and battered notebooks. "I really thought he'd be here," I say, putting down my fork. Julia shrugs. It's my birthday and everything's on hold between me and Perry, of course. But still. I just thought he would be. I reach up and take off my necklace. I look at the little heart and slip it into my pocket.

"Is it time?"

"I think so," I say, looking at the unzipped backpack, dropped there in a hurry as Perry was racing out the door, on to his new adventures.

I ride my board back to the house with half a layer cake. I climb upstairs and call Perry's cell, but it goes to voice mail.

"Perry, hi. It's me. Skate. Listen, the answer is no. It

has to be. It's not going to work with us." My voice catches as I see my bare neck in the mirror. "I still love you a little. But I can't."

I crawl beneath the covers. Tomorrow I'm seventeen. I feel like I've lived three lifetimes already. This must be what it means to grow old. To feel so many things that it hardly makes sense. It seems so long ago since Perry loved me like a crazy man.

The phone rings, and it's him. "I know, Skate," he says.

"You do?" Part of me hoped he'd try to talk me out of it.

"Listen. I changed my schedule. Lightened my load for the spring because I wound up with a C-minus in calculus. So I'm only taking three classes and I'll take two this summer. I also got a job painting dorms, so I'll be in New Brunswick most of the summer, except weekends."

"But Perry, what if I said yes? What if I decided yes?"

"Then we'd work it out somehow." I hear voices in the background. He sighs. "But the point is, you said no. Maybe I knew you would."

"Are you and your girlfriend still together?"

"Yes," he says simply. Nothing else. Then, "Happy birthday, Skate. I still love you a little too."

Barney needs a walk, so I take him. The cold wind feels good on my hot face. Then I get ready for work. Rosie comes in as I'm brushing my hair into a ponytail and sees my necklace on the dresser. "Oh," she says sadly.

"I'm okay," I say.

"Oh," she says again, her eyes filling with tears.

"Really," I say. "Really." I thought it might feel more dramatic but it doesn't. I open my jewelry box and drop the necklace inside and shut the lid.

Barney's gotten big, and he's learning to run beside me on my board. Soon I think we'll be able to make the whole trip to the Heights like that. For now, I ride, he runs, then we slow down for a stretch. It means it takes a while. But I have a lot on my mind, so it's okay.

I drop Barney off at Frank's and spend a few minutes with Lorry before heading to the arcade. Frank's been grocery shopping and the counter is loaded with spices, canned tomatoes, flour. Tonight he's going to cook us dinner and then we'll head up to the boardwalk for the fireworks.

The arcade is hopping this afternoon. With kids off from school and people off from work, we're busy all day. When it slows down, I look at myself in the mirrored wall of the Love Meter and touch my bare neck for a second. But then I get back to work. I collect tickets and hand out yo-yos and mood rings and vampire teeth. Someone even has enough tickets for the toaster oven. It takes me and Frank over a half hour to count them.

"Cha-ching, cha-ching," Frank says as the day winds

down. "Hey, listen. Did I tell you to wear a dress tonight?"

"What?"

"I'm making lobster, did I tell you? So wear a dress, LD."

I laugh. "Sorry, Frank, I don't own a dress. I have a couple, you know, sundresses. But that's it."

"Scrounge one up."

"Oh, please!" I say. "Hey, are we really having lobster?"

"Yes, we are." He smiles. "It's a New-Year's-Eve-Skate's-birthday-eve lobster fest."

"Cool," I say, getting hungry.

"So go now," he says, pulling out the cash tray to count it. "Go beg, borrow, or steal. Scat."

"Yeah, and what are you wearing?"

"My tux, naturally," he says, looking at me. And I know he will, which makes me laugh. Frank's been to so many proms he bought himself a tux a couple years ago.

Perry and I blew off his senior prom. Instead we surfed till sundown, grilled hamburgers and hot dogs on his deck, took blankets up to the dunes, and spent the night naked under the stars. So what do I own? A wet suit, yes. A bathing suit, yes. My birthday suit, yes. But no gown.

Rosie knows just the thing. She digs in her closet, where she has a bunch of poufy party things. She has clothes from our mom and clothes from thrift shops, and she pulls out a long black strapless velvet dress. It's a little bit crushed in places, but it's something. "Try it," she says.

I peel off my clothes and try it on. It's a little big on top. My boobs aren't as big as my mom's were, I guess. So Rosie safety-pins it and I let my hair down. The dress nips in at the waist and fits a little snugly down my legs. There's a slit on either side.

"Wowee," Rosie says, clapping her hands together. Angie pokes her head in and whistles.

"But I don't have shoes."

Turns out Rosie's foot is too big and Angie's too small. No matter. I decide to wear my flip-flops. And I drape a white boa around my neck, one of my - thrift-shop finds. Rosie giggles. "You *have* to go some- where."

"Nope. Just dinner at Frank's, then the boardwalk."

"Too bad," Rosie says, looking all glowy. She tells me about her night: a special New Year's Eve Drama Queen, then a party at Gus's, then up to the boardwalk for the fireworks. Angie's happy too. A couple friends of hers are visiting from Florida. They've been cooking all afternoon. They'll eat and hang out and then also head up to the boardwalk.

I paint my toenails lavender and put on some lip gloss, and then I have to bundle up. I put on tights and my jacket, scarf, hat, and boots. I strap on my backpack and have to hike the dress up to my knees to ride my board, but soon enough I'm good to go.

I reassemble myself on Frank's stoop, tugging off the tights and boots and putting on my flip-flops. I want to make a splashy entrance. "Look what I scrounged up," I'll say, twirling my boa.

The puppies bark and jump all over me. Frank stands at the stove in his sweats and slippers, battling with the live lobsters.

"Ta-da," I say, flapping into the kitchen.

Frank stares at me for a second, the lobster in his hand madly waving its antennae.

"So," I say.

"Well, well . . . ," he says slowly. "LD," he says.

I twirl and my flip-flop squeaks on the linoleum. "And where is your tux?" I say.

"I'm cooking here, my friend. All in good time." He stares at me and smiles, a little smile that I can't quite read but that makes me laugh under my breath.

Frank has outdone himself. Lobster in butter sauce and homemade mini spinach-and-cheese ravioli and a Caesar salad. So we chow down. Frank cracks open a lobster claw and the juice shoots me in the arm. "Hey," I yell. He tosses me a plastic bib decorated with lobsters doing the tango. He puts one on too, over his tux.

"Okay, maybe this wasn't such a hot idea," he says, pulling off his bow tie. He cracks open another claw and squirts me in the face.

"I think you're doing that on purpose, dude."

"I am so totally not doing that on purpose." He tries to crack gently and still manages to squirt me. I squirt him back.

So we crack open the claws—spraying each other and laughing—then dip the meat in butter and suck it down. So totally yum.

When we've made a serious dent in our dinner, I take off my bib. Frank says "Hey—" as he notices my missing necklace. I touch my naked neck.

"Yeah," I say.

Frank watches me, waiting for me to say more, I guess. But there's really nothing more to say. So he goes back to his lobster tail, scooping out the meat. He smiles to himself and dips the meat in butter and holds it over my head like I'm a seal. I tilt my head back, open my mouth, and he drops it in.

When we're done, a pile of shells litters the table. I drape myself across the couch like a jellyfish blob, and Frank heaves himself into the recliner. "Heaven," he sighs.

"I'm never eating again," I lie.

"Not for the next two hours, anyway. There's ice cream for dessert. Sprinkles too."

We stay like that for a while and then do a round of dishes so we don't have to face a total mess tomorrow.

Before midnight Frank takes the puppies out while I bundle up, and then he and I trek up to the boardwalk. It's snowing. Big fat flakes whirl in the air as we find a spot on the pier. Mikey hands around blankets, and Frank takes one. Rosie and Nick, huddled in their jackets and hoods, make their way over, and Angie and her friends, wearing glittery paper tiaras and blowing noisemakers, find us too.

"Oh, look," Rosie says.

The big Ferris wheel lights up and begins to turn. "Come on!" I say.

"Nah," Frank says when I give him a tug. Nick shakes his head.

"I'll puke," says Angie. So Rosie and I run to get in line. Free rides tonight. We scramble into a car, facing each other, and we're lifted oh-so-gently into the night. On the next go-round we stop at the top of the ride while snow blows around us and into the car. Rosie catches some flakes in her glove.

"What's going to happen to us, Skate?" she whispers. "Tell me about the new year." She sits there in her furry hood, looking big-eyed and eager.

"You're the girl with the fortunes. You tell me."

"As a matter of fact . . ." She pulls the stash out of her pocket. "Pick a card, any card." She fans out the pack. "You know it's going to be good, 'cause they're all good." We laugh.

"All right then," I say, plucking a card.

Beat on, my heart!

"Well," Rosie says, looking a little disappointed. "That's not exactly what I had in mind for the New Year."

"It doesn't exactly have pizzazz," I say.

"A little pizzazz would be good. Try again," she says, thrusting the cards at me.

"No, *I'll* tell you how it's gonna be. We're—"

"Wait!" Rosie cries. She scrambles over to my side of the car, rocking us back and forth, and reaches for my hand. "Now tell me."

A little pizzazz, a little zing . . . But I can't think of anything that's not corny, and I want to be real. And something predictable like *We'll be just fine,* while true—absolutely—is definitely lacking in the pizzazz department and not enough for a snowy Ferris wheel ride on the last night of the year.

"Well?" Rosie says.

"Just shush and look," I say, giving her hand a squeeze. So as the wheel turns we look out at the shoreline—the lit-up lighthouse blinking in the distance, the stretch of sand leading to the dark glimmering water, the lit-up pier beneath us, where Angie tips up her face and waves to us and one of her friends tries to get Frank to put on a paper hat, and Nick laughs with Gus. We twist in our seats and look out over the bay, where a boat moves steadily toward the marina, and in the background a million lights shine and twinkle on the mainland.

Rosie smiles and I do too, and when the wheel carries us down we step off without a word.

We join the others as Mikey pops open champagne and hands around little plastic cups. We count down, and toast each other. It's the end of the year and the start of a new one. What's not to like about that? And it's my birthday. I'm seventeen, which seems far from sixteen, even if it's only a single year. The sky above the ocean fills with small bursts of shooting fireworks—blue, green, red, and pink—while the snow continues to fall. I shiver next to Frank, and he wraps me in a blanket. The finale is golden bursts, one little pop after another, some fizzling before they open.

"Lame," Frank sings in my ear.

"Oh, shut up," I say happily. Below us the dark water rolls onto the shore while up here the crowd huddles together on the pier, watching the pops and bursts and little fizzles light the night sky.

The puppies sleep in a little heap by the kitchen door. Frank changes into a T-shirt and sweats and makes us bowls of ice cream complete with a squirt of whipped cream and chocolate sprinkles, and we sit in front of

Dick Clark's Rockin' Eve and eat. And New Year's Eve is over. As fast as that.

I hear Frank brushing his teeth as I make up the couch with the sheets and the soft blue blanket. I take off my heavy tights and boots, but I'm not ready to slip out of the dress. So I crawl beneath the covers with it on and finger my bare neck. I wonder where Perry is tonight and what he's doing. I wonder whether my mother ever wore this dress. I should ask my dad. He might know. If he can remember.

Frank pads over to me and hangs over the couch. "Happy birthday, Skate."

I reach up and touch his arm. "Thank you."

"For what?"

And I'm ready to rattle off a list that's grown long. But I stare at his sleepy face. "Just for everything."

"Okay," he says. He pads off to his room, and I hear the squeak of his mattress as he drops down.

"Angie and Rosie are making brunch in the morning, if you want to come over with me."

"Oh, okay." He yawns.

"Omelets, I think. All kinds of omelets, and fresh-squeezed orange juice, and they've been baking too. Coffee cake. Cheesecake . . ." Frank flips off his lamp and his room goes completely dark. "Are you listening?"

"Nope." I hear another yawn.

"How come you didn't ask me about Perry?"

" 'Cause I think I know."

"What do you know?"

"Why is it you get all chitchatty when I'm about to drop?"

"It's my birthday," I say, sitting up, not feeling the least bit tired. But I hear him yawn again. "Frank? Are you sleeping?"

"Yup."

I get up and dig my slippers out of the hall closet. I brush my teeth and loop my hair into a messy ponytail and wash my face. Still in my gown, I stand in his doorway and listen, but I can't tell if he's asleep or not. So I creep over and sit on the edge of the bed. "Hey, Frank," I say softly.

"Hey," he says, rolling over, and I can see him smiling in the dark.

"Hey."

"So, how's it going, LD?" he asks, propping his head on his hand.

"Can I just lie down with you? For a little while?"

He holds open the blanket and I slip inside with my back to him, and he spoons around me all toasty warm.

"What do you know?" I ask. "About Perry?"

"That it's *finito*. You took off the necklace."

"Yep," I say quietly. "So how come you're not bugging me about you and me? Or did you get over that idea already? Is there another LD already in the wings?"

"Um, excuse me," he whispers into my neck. "But

who did I have dinner with on the last night of the year? Who do I own puppies with? Who did I make lobsters in butter sauce for? Who did I schlep up to the board-walk with to watch the lame-o fireworks? Huh?" He lets out a long lazy yawn, kind of bored-sounding, and I laugh out loud.

"You're so romantic, Frank."

"But I am, LD. I am. Just you wait."

"For what?"

"For what's next."

"What's that?"

"Me and you. Naturally." And he kisses me on the ear.

And I'm ready to say, *You can do better than that, pal.* But it's enough for right now. I take Frank's hand and he loops his fingers through mine. And we fall asleep just like that.

Beth Ann Bauman is the author of a short story collection for adults, *Beautiful Girls,* and the recipient of a New York Foundation for the Arts fellowship. Growing up, she spent summers on the Jersey shore. She now lives in New York City.